DUST
EUGENE
TODDLER ON THE RUN

These two punchy, vivid novellas show Shena Mackay's inimitable skill in recording the lives of the urban dispossessed – the young men and women who kick against an authority that besieges them. Abigail pines for her lover during school assemblies where nuns preach sacrifice, but romance is snatched from them when he crashes the car stolen for their joy-ride. With Eugene sent down for two years, she has ample opportunity to pursue adolescent angst and to contemplate his escape... Morris, twenty-three years old and only three feet nine inches tall, is often mistaken for a child, though the events that entangle him are far from childish. On the run from the law he takes refuge in a beach hut with Leda. Camouflaged by donkey rides and festive holiday-makers, they scramble through the days, fortified by salty tea, beset with fear and desperation.

SHENA MACKAY

Shena Mackay was born in Edinburgh. She is the author of two novellas, three collections of short stories and seven novels. Her novel *Dunedin* and the collection of short stories, *The Laughing Academy*, both won Scottish Arts Council Book Awards and the bestselling *Orchard On Fire* was shortlisted for the 1996 Booker Prize and the McVitie's Prize. She lives in London.

BY SHENA MACKAY

Shena Mackay

DUST FALLS ON EUGENE SCHLUMBURGER

TODDLER ON THE RUN

V

VINTAGE

Published by Vintage 1998

2 4 6 8 10 9 7 5 3 1

First published in Great Britain by
André Deutsch Limited in 1964

Vintage
Random House, 20 Vauxhall Bridge Road,
London SW1V 2SA

Random House Australia (Pty) Limited
20 Alfred Street, Milsons Point, Sydney
New South Wales 2061, Australia

Random House New Zealand Limited
18 Poland Road, Glenfield,
Auckland 10, New Zealand

Random House South Africa (Pty) Limited
Endulini, 5A Jubilee Road, Parktown 2193,
South Africa

Random House UK Limited Reg. No. 954009

A CIP catalogue record for this book
is available from the British Library

ISBN 0 09 927075 7

Papers used by Random House UK Ltd are natural,
recyclable products made from wood grown in sustain-
able forests. The manufacturing processes conform to the
environmental regulations of the country of origin

Printed and bound in Great Britain by
Cox & Wyman, Reading, Berkshire

Shena Mackay

DUST FALLS ON
EUGENE SCHLUMBURGER

Dust Falls on Eugene Schlumburger

[1]

Eugene woke in a paper hat and went to the window where it was snowing.

Snow was falling on the rabbit hutch and on the thin cat, on the broken saucer and on the abandoned tricycle. A bottle he had brought from the party lay broken, half-filled with snow. Still in pyjamas, he went down to the yard. It was eleven o'clock and the washing was frozen on the line. Eugene shook the line so that the clothes jumped stiffly in a thin shower of snow. 'Christians, Awake!' sang Eugene, and the clothes danced.

A face in sunglasses appeared at the kitchen window.

'Merry Christmas, Mrs Mayhew,' called Eugene. The eyes behind the sunglasses suffered and a thin voice said: 'I've got one of my awful migraine headaches,' and in a flurry of dusters the face disappeared.

He went back to bed and closed his eyes between the shivering whiteness of the twisted sheets and thought back to the night before.

It was the second night of the party. He stood swaying in the doorway. In the half-darkened room reclining couples filled the floor. He saw across the room a girl lying prone beside a man. In the bad smoky light all he could see clearly was her feet because she had kicked her shoes off. They lay white and mournful on the carpet. Eugene stood with tears jumping to his eyes as he looked at her worn and vulnerable white feet.

He walked towards her through a group discussing

1

laconically the bomb which would bring the final annihilation of all the tired feet.

The record player stopped. He saw she was flicking cigarette ash into the hair of a sleeping bearded boy. He sat down beside her, and said: 'This party's a washout.'

'You shouldn't have said that.'

'Why not?'

'Because until somebody says "This party's a flop" you can pretend you're having a wonderful time.'

'Why pretend?'

He led her out into the pure snow. It was Christmas Eve. Behind him he heard the lonely sound of a man being sick.

Eugene heard the sound of quiet sobbing coming from Davis's room. The door was ajar so he went in. Davis was wiping his eyes.

'Christmas has been spoiled,' he said. 'The Christmas card I gave Mrs Mayhew is in the wastepaper basket. It was such a pretty card, and she does like budgies. But there's always someone who spoils Christmas. Every year since I was a boy I always hoped that they wouldn't, but they do. One year I dreamed I dropped my stocking and all my presents were broken. I couldn't even open my stocking after that. I didn't want to because it had been spoiled already.'

Eugene, standing on one leg in drooping pyjamas, said: 'I would ask you into my room for a Christmas drink but I know you don't drink and the place is in rather a mess. Anyway, Merry Christmas, and thanks for the card.'

The truth was he couldn't let Davis enter his room and see the card wasn't displayed. But Davis, the biggest spoiler of them all, was inside the room, disappointment in his eyes. Eugene ran to a drawer and pulled out a handful of cards which he put on the mantelpiece.

'I like to keep my cards clean,' he lied.

[2]

The fallen petals of pink Christmas roses lay on the
table and the wind moaned outside. Night was a square
of black in the window. Davis, who was a doorkeeper at
the Silver Vaults, crouched in a chair, saying: 'God
knows I've suffered' with his head in his hands. Mrs
Mayhew came in and swept up the petals and Davis
burst into tears. Crying for the desolate wind and the
fallen petals. Crying because the spoiling of Christmas
was left to a menial like Mayhew, because there was
no one else.

After a bit he dried his eyes in front of the mirror and
took out a yellow notebook, a wooden pen and a bottle
of purple ink. 'The tools of my trade,' thought Davis,
and he began to write. Once he got up to eat an apple,
then he stared out of the window for a bit. It didn't open
but you got a nice view if you held the curtains back.
Pale green lamps hung in the dark blue sky, and all was
quiet except faraway traffic, and the snow fluttered
like green moths round the streetlights.

At ten o'clock he tore a page from his notebook and
copied out neatly what he had written. He would show
it to Mrs Mayhew who had recently had a cat put to sleep.

'We've kept your empty basket
And your fav'rite collar, dear.
But now our hearts are lonesome
And we're wishing you were here.

A place we'll keep within our hearts,
A place that's true and sound,
Until once more we meet you, Jock,
In the Happy Hunting Ground.'

Davis felt elevated.

'Gene,' he called, tapping on the thin dividing wall, 'I wonder if you'd step in here a moment.'

Eugene came in, smudge-eyed from reading in the dim light. He was without shoes.

'What's all this?' he asked, pointing to the pen, ink and notebook.

'The Tools of my Trade,' said Davis.

Eugene read the poem and handing it back reverently, said: 'It is very sad. But very true. All human life is there, as it were.' He left the room, much affected.

Davis put his poem with a covering letter in an envelope addressed to *Pet's Own Magazine* and went bed.

The bed was cold and uncomfortable. Davis always took food with him to bed and biscuit crumbs caused him much pain. Tonight he had an orange and the juice ran down his sleeves.

[3]

Tonight he was meeting that girl from the party. This was Eugene's last thought at night and almost his first on waking. Snow lay thinly on the roofs with etchings of birds' feet scratched on its surface. He liked to think of birds walking above him as he slept.

A few months earlier Eugene had won an architecture competition which had enabled him to leave his job in an advertising agency and live in temporary retirement in Mrs Mayhew's boarding house in Victoria. He reckoned the money should last him at least another three months.

It was ten o'clock. Eugene fried an egg and read yesterday's *Evening News*. Davis had gone to work and Mrs Mayhew was shopping. The house was quiet except that the West Indian students downstairs were playing records. Eugene stood in his doorway listening. They had mostly old records. It was as if someone had given them his record collection when he ceased to be a teenager a couple of years ago.

> 'The night is so lonely
> And I dream of you only'

That fragment was all he could remember of it afterwards, but he was singing it all day.

It was too cold to go out. Eugene lay in front of the electric fire and listened to the wireless. Mrs Dale had rather a cold and spoke in a hoarse whisper. Jim was very busy with 'flu patients, but took time off for coffee and cattiness to Mary and Mother-in-law. There was something a bit sinister about Jim: one felt that consulting room could tell some tales. In a vague way he reminded Eugene of the Duke of Edinburgh.

That girl was called Abigail and she was sixteen and thin with long red hair with sparks of gold in it.

'The day is so lonely and I dream of you only', thought Eugene with his eyes shut in front of the fire.

Abigail saw Eugene first. He was standing by the bookstall at Charing Cross, wearing narrow green corduroy trousers, a white mac and suède boots. She stood beside him for perhaps two minutes before he saw her. When he did, his lazy eyes lit up and he smiled, elusive like a cat.

They went to the News Theatre at Leicester Square. Eugene felt happier than he had for months and looking at Abigail believed the same of her. Especially the Three Stooges were funny. They saw the programme twice. Abigail found that Eugene had neat hairy hands with a gold ring on the third finger of his right hand.

When they came out she said: 'Do you know, I've never laughed at the Three Stooges before. Have you?'

'Never.'

Night was circling in great stars round Nelson's Column, snow falling and filling the fountains, breaking in silver stars upon the watery spears and the dolphins' green mouths. They sat on the edge of a fountain. Hoar frost sparkled on the stone rim where they sat.

Two policemen stamped round the square and an old

7

Indian trailed broken footsteps past them, shivering as the snow filled his shoes, slowly, from the sole.

As the policeman's boots faded in the softness behind the plinth he took her in his arms.

'O, Gene, Gene, Eugene, darling, you have a ribcage like an ox.'

'Sheep may safely graze' tinkled through the dark unlit hall and down the corridor. Two ivory arms hovered above the yellow keyboard and old stained ivory hands grazed quietly among the keys. On one finger was a jade ring.

The light was switched on and girls filed in, little girls lumpy and thin and big girls lumpy and thin until the hall was full of girls with vegetable legs in socks.

The piano teacher gathered up her hands and hymnbook and sat back on her stool, waiting.

The hall door opened and Miss Benthall entered. The head girl followed with a hymnbook.

'Hymn Number two hundred and twenty-six – 2–2–6.'

> 'Eternal Father, strong to save,
> Whose arm doth bind the restless wave,
> Who bids the mighty ocean deep
> Its own appointed limits keep.
> Oh, hear us when we cry to thee
> For those in peril on the sea.'

Snow was still falling past the window and the sky was as grey as lead. A black tree waved against the window and the goalposts creaked in the yellow mud of the hockey-pitch and the wind moaned in the nets.

Six hundred schoolgirls praying for sailors. Schoolgirls in collars and ties singing of sailors in the hard electric glare of the depth of winter.

'—when my ship comes home I'll bring you a sari from India. Wait for me, Abigail.'

'Yes, I'll wait for you. I'll write you a letter to every part.'

'Do you love me, Abigail?'

'You know I do, Johnny.'

And then in the dark behind the Portsmouth Odeon: 'Yes, Johnny, yes . . .'

> – To give and not to count the cost
> To fight and not to heed the wounds
> To toil and not to seek for rest
> To labour and not to ask for any reward
> Save that of knowing that we do thy will
> A – A – Amen.
> Descant Amen by the choir.

'And now let us pray for the County Councils of this realm . . .'

Abigail thought: snow is filling the hockey nets and glittering on the yellow mud, freezing the drive and filling the hedges. Mounting in desolation on the windowsills, wailing at the pane, drifting under doors. Soon it will cover the desks and the algebra books, fill the crucible and the belljar and thoroughly obliterate the blackboard. Blue glaciers will form in the inkwells. Perhaps Benthall's car will skid on the drive and hurtle in frozen flames through the hollyhedge. Supposing they all broke their legs on the hockey pitch. 'Bully off!' and they charged, and their legs broke like hockeysticks, their faces like netballs sank into the snow.

'The Under Thirteen Netball team lost 5 to 3 to the Sacred Heart Under Thirteens, the Under Fifteens won 4 to 2 and the Over Fifteens lost 9 to 3. Well done, Under Fifteens!'

Puny applause.

'And now from something pleasant to something less pleasant. I want these three girls to come up on the platform: Janice Webb, Dolores Kellog, Mavis Sloat.'

To the faint minstrelsy of blowing noses and filing nails three white-faced prisoners walked down the gangway and mounted the dock. Heads screwed round and teachers, too, craned forward as at a public execution. The piano teacher sat on her hands.

'These girls, all fourth year leavers, beat up – yes, you may well gasp – beat up a second year girl on the way home from school last night. In addition to this display of utter bestiality, there are no other words to describe it . . .'

The voice rose to a shriek and, her fat figure shaking with rage in her gown, she pointed the finger of accusation at the prisoners.

' . . . In addition to this bestiality, not one of these girls was wearing her beret. These girls, I call them girls for want of a better word, these girls shall learn that violence reaps a reward of recrimination. They will not be rejoining their classes. They have disgraced their parents and the School. Look at them, and be warned. They are guttersnipes and shall be dealt with as such.'

She flung out of the shocked and silent hall.

The Head Girl read out the Lost Property Notices.

The pianoforte teacher was back at the piano, her eyes fixed on pastures beyond the snow, while her old

11

white hands strayed bleating over the keys. The games teacher beat time on a hymnbook at the door.

Mavis Sloat twisted a handkerchief in her hand but her arms were paralysed. She couldn't reach her face. Dolores Kellog giggled hopelessly. The hall emptied and the music stopped. Someone switched off the lights. The three white-faced figures stood in a row on the platform and faced the empty rows of chairs. It was a full minute before they could look at each other or climb down.

Class Five A was back in the form room.

'They ought to be beaten up themselves publicly,' said Marion Bethel.

'Bloody stupid bitch.'

'You want to wash your mouth out with soap and water, Abigail Fawkes.'

'Marion Bethel lives in a brothel, Marion Bethel lives in a brothel, Marion Bethel lives in a brothel,' mocked Abigail and her friend, Jane.

'O, belt up,' said Marion reaching for her hockey boots.

Gaudy figures splotched on the yellow mud and splayed in the positions of hockey. Divots of frozen grass lifted into the metal sky as racing blue legs in red socks churned the pitch, purple hands flailing frozen sticks.

The secretary came carefully in mock leopard-skin boots over the planks that spanned the worst of the mud.

'O, Miss Hatcher, can you spare a moment? Abigail Fawkes's uncle has telephoned to say her mother is ill. Miss Benthall would like to see Abigail now.'

Miss Hatcher, a cheerful contrast in her gay scarlet

tracksuit and sheepskin mitts to the frozen girls in shorts and aertex blouses, assented. Abigail left the field aware of sympathetic eyes accompanying her.

But the eyes which faced her across the rosewood desk were not sympathetic.

'Your Uncle Eugene wants you to go home. I hardly think this is necessary but he was very insistent. You may go home but I expect you to be back tomorrow. Tell your mother, whom, I may add, I have never had the pleasure of meeting at any of our socials, that I hope she will soon be well. And don't forget to collect your homework before you go.'

Abigail ran down the drive. A figure stepped out from the hedge in front of her.

'Eugene! You made me jump.'

'Sorry, love. The car's round the corner. Are you hungry? There's some sweets in the car or we could have a drink somewhere.'

'I'm starving. But let's get out of here quick. This place stinks.'

[5]

Eugene sat with his hands on the steering wheel, like a mole in his brown corduroy suit. The black Wolseley skidded into the car park of the 'Red Hand of Ulster'. He got out and held the door open but Abigail didn't move.

'I can't go in there, Gene.'

'Why not?'

'I'll look pretty moronic in a pub in school uniform.'

'Christ! Yes. Wait here and I'll bring something out.'

It was freezing in the car. The heater was broken. Abigail sat on her feet to hatch them into warmth. Eugene seemed hours. She twisted a knob in the front of the car – the radio was broken too.

Eugene crossed the car park with snow in his ears and a bottle in his hand and peanuts in his pockets.

'There's some peanuts in my pocket. This ought to warm you up.' He gave her a small bottle of Black and White.

The initial excitement of the illicit ride had worn off and Eugene and Abigail felt a profound tangible melancholy rise up between them as they drove through silent lanes, sullen and shadowed with snow. The narrow roads and even the car made no noise and they drove on in silence.

Suddenly something ran across the road in front of the car. Eugene braked. The car slid to a stop.

'What was it, Eugene?'

'I don't know. I suppose I'd better look.'

'I suppose so.'

Eugene got out of the car and quenched his cigarette. There was a bright hot stain under the front wheel. A still brown rag of fur lay between the front wheels.

'God, it's still alive. Abby, help me quick.'

Eugene lifted gently, with sickness in his mouth, the rabbit and laid him in Abigail's lap. The stain spread to her skirt. He lay with his soft ears laid back, watching out of troubled eyes.

For a minute his head turned backwards and he jerked, heartbeats jarring his warm body. Then his eyes glazed. He slid gently and so neatly into death. Death fitted him like a glove.

Eugene took the long soft paws and crossed them on the white breast. He saw they were all worn out with digging, poor worn out sad sand-stained paws. They scratched a shallow grave with the handle of a comb. Benedicite, rabbit – it is the final covering over that is the most appalling.

Abigail's eyes were choked with glacial tears.

'Look at my bloody skirt. Eugene, supposing his wife was pregnant? Cover up the stain.'

[6]

Later that evening. Shielded by his heroic arm against the unloveliness of night, circled in his velvet fur, her heart knotted with love, Abigail lay in the paws of a mole. Eugene lay white and starry sinewed with his ragged dark head on her bent arm and his leg between hers.

'Eugene, did you know you're a mole?'

'A mole?' I always saw myself as some kind of bird – but perhaps you're right. Yes – I think you are.'

Her hair lay in thick snakes on the pillow and her eyes glittered like a golden snake's eyes.

'You know,' she said, 'I never thought I could love someone so much. I used to see myself as a rather solitary lady with short grey hair, striding alone on the moors, communing with nature bareheaded in the storm – and perhaps tending a few simple herbs. Or else a bundle of rags on a park bench.'

When Eugene put on his jacket his wallet fell out of the pocket.

Abigail picked it up.

'Who's that?' she said, pointing to a photograph of an unsmiling girl with straight black hair. She spoke calmly but her heart turned right over.

'That? Oh, it's a girl called Angela. Do you want to tear it up?'

Abigail was appalled. 'How can you be so cruel. You

must have loved her once. You can't just destroy a person like that.'

'I never loved her. It was only lust. She was a rejected kind of girl, and I felt sorry for her.'

'I'm not rejected.'

'I still love you.'

The moon was sailing in veils of snow across the whirling sky among the snapping snouts of the stars. Shooting stars scattered and broke in trails of light blown by the black east wind.

Eugene in a sheepskin and Abigail in a corduroy coat came down the steps with their collars turned up against the bitter wind. They walked huddled together to the top of the hill. All day children had been making a slide down the steep pavement which bent sharply at an almost right angle about a hundred yards from the bus stop.

Abigail broke loose from the encircling arms and began sliding and spiralling down the hill until all Eugene could see in the moonlight was her red hair spinning into the white eternity. He started to run but his legs were heavy with cold and snowflakes melted in his eyes blinding him. He ran, heavy and lost, his hard feet pounding the slithering ground. Then he tripped on a lump of ice and fell, hitting his face on the kerb. The sky flashed round his head and he lay there for a minute, his cut face bleeding into the snow, and desolation in his heart feeling he had lost her forever. He raised his weak legs and tried to walk, but his steps degenerated into a slide. As he cruised unsteadily round the corner, he saw himself as she would in a second – 'I am a man of thirty sliding in the snow with blood on my face.'

She stood at the bus stop, her hair spiked with snow-flakes, waiting for him. She wiped his face with her hair because she had no handkerchief. As the bus drew away a street lamp lit the face of a battered mole.

[7]

Our Lady of the Sorrows' bells ring brokenly through the dripping woods. Wet leaves have choked the clappers and the bells mumble like old sisters at Mass. Two lights burn in the dark institution, one in the chapel and the other, high in the grey wall, flutters from a narrow window. An old woman stands at the window holding a fox fur. Grey hair twists on her shoulders like dead eels and half covers a white sunken face. Her eyes reflect light like broken glass. She is Davis's sister.

'Tonight the wet mournful wind is sobbing in the gargoyles' broken mouths. Before my mouth was broken, one October night when I was walking in the dripping woods, a man was waiting for me underneath the trees. The moon fell slanting on his face and his arms were as soft as paws. I screamed, but a bird rose and stopped my throat. The eyes of a fox, neither startled nor sly, lay silent as stones under a close-by bush.

'My brother, who came here quickly with a kiss, and soon left in a taxi, left me this fur that I cannot wear. O, fox, they have taken your moonstone eyes and only your sad dangling paws remember the dripping woods. I would take you to the woods but the windows are barred and only an cccasional leaf drifts over the mossy wall.

'The sisters cross themselves and mutter in the chapel. If this snow continues the carp pond will

19

over-flow and fish float through the orchard, brown fish and yellow apples collide in the floating frozen black orchard.

'Even now in the sacristy Sister Mary Joseph is mustering nets.

'O, Fox in my arms at the dark window pane, I hear him push his leafy bicycle through the dripping woods again—'

Sister Matthias has girded up her loins to reveal thighs. She is wearing wellingtons and her coarse serge cassock is draggled with mud. A moribund carp, held by the tail, its bright scales slurred with blood, twitches from either bony hand. She slits and cleans them with a cruciform knife, whistling a descant to one of the lesser known psalms.

A pan is boiling on the stove. It contains five cut-up eels and Sister Matthias throws in the mutilated carp.

She is of an unpleasing countenance, sallow, with broken purple contour lines shaping irregular hillocks of grief. She sighs as she thinks of the whip: it is not a sigh of pain, rather, the timeless longing of the tomb.

Our Lady of the Sorrows' Convent was intended to house the insane and similar pariahs of the parish, and it had had its heyday, but times have changed and now the sisters care for only Davis, and she is not of this parish.

> 'A valiant woman, we proclaim,
> Whose constancy her sex belied.
> Clear as the sun her virtue's fame
> And as the earth itself is wide.'

Enter Sister Matthias bearing aloft the bowl of fish

soup. Triumphant steam forms a transitory halo above her head – she is Salome with the charger.

'Sister Matthias! Is it fitting, deem you, thus to appear before your Maker at His bountiful banquet?'

The bowl crashes to the floor and eel and carp are swilled on the floor with dark brown liquid. Her distracted hands fly from her boots to her thighs, to her boots. The soup steams slowly through her horror-struck feet.

'If Our Lord had meant us to come into His presence in wellingtons, He would have given us rubber feet. Sister Matthias! You will not attend bell-ringing, flagellation or any other recreation for three weeks. Make your peace with God!'

> 'Praise to the Father, as is meet,
> Praise to the sole begotten Son,
> Praise to the Holy Paraclete,
> While everlasting ages run.'

The Sisters rise and file out of the refectory. The youngest novice bursts into tears of frustrated hunger – for which twelve Paternosters is just recompense.

Prostrate before the altar Sister Matthias hears with groans laughter and the swishing whips.

'Just my luck,' she mutters, as her gumboots make a dismal fire upon the altar of her shame.

[8]

Davis sighed as he slit open the envelope addressed in pencil and bearing two threepenny stamps. Inside was a Holy Picture on the back of which was printed in pencil:

AT HOME

Miss Ellen Davis
on Saturday
Bring your friends to Our
Lady of the Sorrows at 3 pm

On Saturday Davis, Eugene and Abigail walked dismally through the great iron gate. Davis had on a Homburg hat, Abigail was wearing a black skirt and sweater and Eugene's sheepskin coat, and Eugene was a mole. The others stood on the third stone step while Davis rang the bell.

'Joseph Davis and party,' said Davis briskly to the white face that appeared at the grille and the door swung open. They followed her silent figure through heavy corridors paved with broken tears, the keys at her girdle jangling against the sound of distant singing in stone walls and the east wind in the spires.

Ellen Davis stood in her doorway in a mantle of dull green silk which fell in opaque folds to the ground. White sapphires burned at her throat and wrists. She kissed Davis and Eugene and shook hands with Abigail.

'First, my dears,' hooking an arm round Davis's waist, 'a little entertainment I have devised for you.' She drew back the serge curtain and beckoned her guests to the window. They had a clear view of a little cemetery, liberally sprinkled with homemade crosses and an occasional wooden dove. Wreaths of snow decked stone cherubs' smiling heads and filled their cracked mouths.

Even as they watched the sky grew dark.

From the little chapel came a procession, slowly, singing. They bore aloft a simple coffin. Sister Agnes led the way with an electric torch.

'It is Sister Sick of the Palsy,' said Ellen Davis through bluish, almost phosphorescent lips.

Was it only in imagination Abigail saw the coffin twitch? On the far side of the cemetery lay a new grave. Slowly the Sisters advanced, singing under the Milky Way, the stars glinting on their creaky boots, their robes brushing the snow from the narrow path.

Suddenly the torchlight flickered and failed. The lamp of their room afforded the watchers light enough to see the pantomime's end but the black figures below seemed plunged into nearly complete darkness. They stumbled on in the direction of the freshly dug grave.

'Lead, Kindly Light, amid the encircling gloom,
 Lead thou me on . . .'

But they took a wrong turning. The Sisters lowered their burden gently over the side, into its narrow house of earth. They let go. There was a terrific splash, several of the Sisters screamed and some were soaked.

'The well!' A despairing cry rose from a dozen

throats. Vainly from the depths the palsied bubbles rose.

'All drinking water must be boiled from now on,' the Mother Superior broke the silence. The Sisters turned and picked their way over slippery tombstones to the cheerful refectory. The thin voice of a novice piped through the still cold air.

> 'The day thou gavest Lord is ended,
> The darkness falls at thy behest.
> To thee our morning hymns ascended,
> Thy praise shall sanctify our rest.'

But in the simple cell now embellished with vomit there was no rest. A fox barked clear and cold from the woods . . . For a second Ellen Davis stood rigid like a tall candle, then she plunged streaming like a shooting star from the window, stars in her loosened hair and the wind in her robe.

They rushed down the stairs and into the cemetery, Davis's screams rousing swarms of nuns who ran with them, holding up their cassocks. It was so dark outside, Davis stood screaming in the blackness until lamps and torches were brought from inside.

Ellen Davis lay broken and jangling in the new grave, the glass of her eyes dulled and her bright mouth dimmed. A trail of paw marks led from the bitter brink towards the woods. Davis knelt in the open grave with her white hand in his purple hands and earth and snow rained on his bowed head and tears rattled down his empty face.

[9]

'It is better so. She was not of this world. Every family has its cross to bear and Ellen was ours.'

Davis stood on the rush mat in the centre of his new room. The floor was pine and scrubbed and beeswaxed so that it shone in the sparkling firelight. He was in white shirt-sleeves and stood with his hands in the pockets of new stiff navy overalls. A folding rule poked out of the long pocket on his leg.

His face was blank like an ironed handkerchief. He did not think often of his sister now. Occasionally when the rainy wind woke him – then he thought of her. Like a light switched off, when he awoke in the morning he forgot. Sometimes after several days' absence she broke into his thoughts like a blunt knife but the tight red uniform had held no aching heart.

A white marble placque lettered in black on the convent wall said:

'Caretaker – J. Davis.'

The caretaker's head, framed in the shining window, watched the Sisters in the Cloisters.

'It is a pity they are either scrubbed faced with glasses or hairy like old goats. Some of them seem to have scrubbed so hard that their faces look like old nailbrushes. Also I think Sister Latimer is missing a leg. Or maybe more.'

The youngest novices, all in their early thirties, were

25

playing leapfrog by the cloister walls: Sister Matthias was playing leapfrog by herself.

Davis had a handy room adjoining Sister Bernadette's cell. Alas for Sister Bernadette! On a pilgrimage to Lourdes with a blind friend she had been knocked down and run over by a wheelchair. She was badly trampled and received a savage blow from a metal crutch.

Her blind friend she never saw again. On the third day of her grimy search, battling against her rainsodden cassock and sleepladen eyes, Sister Bernadette stumbled upon a stall. The smiling stallholder was pointing to his wares, with rivulets of rain running into his ears and from the black points of his hair. Across the stall lay rows and rows of white wooden sticks labelled 'Lourdes Rock'. A little child was sucking one.

It was then all the heart went out of Sister Bernadette and leaning heavily on her makeshift crutches she limped to the coach station.

Davis strolled around the room, putting the finishing touches to it, smoothing his cushion and patting his bed. Then he watered the cactus. A framed copy of his poem, which, incidentally, had been rejected by *Pet's Own Magazine*, hung over the mantelpiece.

[10]

Eugene and Abigail had been out with two of Eugene's friends, Robert and Alberto, and they were at Charing Cross waiting for Abigail's train. The train was not due for another twenty minutes so they went along the Charing Cross embankment and sat on the steps overlooking the river.

Above them the obelisk and below the bitter waters of the Thames. They sat on the first dry step above the yellow water. Driftwood and fishscales and frayed ends of rope slapped the step in the ebb of the London tide. A lighted ship sailed down the river, the foghorn burst the black sky with stars and a bottle thrown from the deck held for a moment a polished replica of the moon.

'At this moment,' Abigail was thinking, 'sitting here with my hands inside his jacket on his ribcage like an ox, the rough jacket on the outside of my hands and beneath them the bones and his heart beating like a giant, if he told me to I would to death walk smiling into the water.'

Just as in her thoughts the black waters closed over her triumphant head, Eugene spoke.

'I read that the highest number of suicides the river police pull out of the river are ageing whores. The only means of identification is their handbags which are found floating at some distance. When they jump they hold their handbags tight because they are all they've got and when they die even the handbags are not faithful.' The ship died slowly in the dark.

'The saddest thing I ever saw,' said Abigail, 'was at Charing Cross Underground. There was this exhibition of mentally handicapped children. You know, photographs of well-integrated Mongol children making sandcastles and spastics climbing trees. I was walking round this exhibition when music started coming through a loudspeaker. It was children's voices high and husky singing "Golden Slumbers". You know:

> "Golden slumbers kiss your eyes,
> Smiles awake you when you rise,
> Sleep, pretty darlings, do not cry
> And I will sing a lullaby." '

As they walked up the platform at Charing Cross, tall scaffolding rose out of the white mist.

After the train, Abigail got on a bus. The lower deck was empty. As she passed the long seat she picked up a folded pink *Evening News* and took it to her seat. When the conductress, a beefy grey-haired woman with a cleft chin and white socks, took her fare, she pointed to a sixpence lying on the seat beside Abigail and took it, saying it was hers. Abigail, counting the change in her hand, knew different.

The bus stopped at some traffic lights. Abigail heard the conductress say: 'It's fascinating to watch a crowd of deaf and dumbs talking, isn't it?'

A passenger assented. On the corner a group of about twelve deaf mutes stood, tapping their fingers, pointing to their mouths, gesticulating and laughing. They were having a good laugh at one of their number who, with one hand in a sling and two fingers missing on the other, was practically bereft of speech.

When she had finished the *Evening News* which contained nothing, she crumpled it up on the seat beside her. In a second, the conductress, claws asunder, was beside her.

'I hope you've quite finished with my newspaper?'

'O – is it yours?'

'Certainly it's mine. Why else would it be folded up on the long seat? You might at least have folded it up again.'

'I might have, but I didn't.'

The conductress held the paper aloft like a tattered pink battle flag, for all the bus to look upon.

Abigail sat and looked out of the window, dreading walking past the conductress and deciding her punishment. She saw herself writing a letter to the London Transport Executive.

'Dear Sir,

As one who fought at Passchendaele, I feel it my duty, and that of every citizen, to protest about the conduct of Bus Conductress CL 27344 on the 46 route.

Last Thursday evening she was both insolent and negligent in her behaviour towards an elderly handicapped person. In fact, if it had not been for the prompt action of a gentleman in the bus queue, the said handicapped lady might have been crushed beneath the wheels of an oncoming lorry.

I was prepared to overlook this but when on the following evening I saw conductress CL 27344 give the wrong change to a blind kiddie, I was spurred to action. Also her language is coarse and her uniform sloppy.

May I be permitted to add that I think the coloured conductors are doing well in a difficult job.

Yours, etc.,

A. Fawkes (retired)'

She saw the conductress, stripped of her uniform, denuded of her cap and sporran, a lonely figure haunting the bus terminus, furtively picking up stray tickets, waiting in vain outside the forbidden canteen door, while the lonely lights of a trolleybus shine in her eyes.

[11]

Redder than holly are Mrs Mayhew's nails. They danced on the counter like circus riders' legs in red high-heeled boots. Her heels scraped the sawdust of the butcher's floor. The butcher put two pigs' trotters in a bag and she gave him the money with a smile.

The pink dancers who first lay in the golden straw and later stood starred with mud in the rain, the double pas-de-deux of a running pig ended, wept blood in the paper bag.

Mrs Mayhew wore a polythene bag on her head to protect her home perm from the sleet but it ran down her face and neck and her red lips itched. She stood for shelter under Campbell the Butcher's awning, after venturing a few steps in the sleet. In the window a full grown pig reclined on a bed of parsley. There was a sprig of parsley in either ear and one hung like a cigarette from the corner of his mouth.

'Mr Campbell's ever so artistic,' thought Mrs Mayhew.

The table was laid for the evening meal and the potatoes were drained and the hot trotters buttered. Mrs Mayhew looked at the green enamel clock – five o'clock.

Then she decided to go ahead with the meal. She heaped potatoes on her plate and added two pigs' feet to the pile. Wiping her lips with a Kleenex tissue, which she threw half-crumpled in an ash-tray, she switched on the television and sat opposite it with a plate on her knee.

As she was eating a shadow flickered across the screen. She turned round just in time to see a pale snout-like face pass the window. Then the door opened. Mrs Mayhew screamed. A pig stood in the doorway on its hind legs. His front hooves were folded on his chest, his lower half was encased in a huge paper bag tied round the waist with string.

'I am looking for my feet,' he said.

When Mrs Mayhew came to she was lying on the floor. The television announcer was saying: '—And now we present "Pygmalion".'

She looked at her plate: he had taken the potatoes as well.

[12]

Outside London Bridge Underground Station a man was playing 'You are my sunshine' on a silver trumpet and when he rested it to blow his frozen fingers, snowflakes drifted into its battered mouth.

As Eugene Schlumburger walked to Bank, slush capped his suède boots with black. He met his friend Charley Baker outside the Chase Manhattan Bank. Charley was wandering driftingly down the street with his hands in his trouser pockets and only a jacket, no coat. He looked a macabre figure leaning against the façade of the Chase Manhattan Bank. Bright flags were blowing from the roofs in the icy wind, stretched across the sky like paper, the star-spangled banner drooped a little in the snow.

They went into a small café which was empty except for the Italian proprietor, who was reading a comic. They slid into a yellow plastic seat. There were red and green plastic tomatoes containing tomato sauce and pink salt and pepper flowers on the yellow speckled tables.

'Two cappucinis,' said Charley, and Eugene hated him. The walls were decorated with archaic 7-Up advertisements. The juke box was dead and it was quiet until the waiter switched on 'Five to ten, a story, a hymn and a prayer.'

Charley's eyes were red-rimmed and his hair was wet and knotted like sheep's wool caught on a fence. As he raised a dirty khaki handkerchief to his face, Eugene saw the sideways glitter of his eyes.

'What's the matter, Charley?'

Charley slurped his coffee. 'I am on my way to the divorce courts. It is an undefended petition on the grounds of adultery.'

'What! Roberta was unfaithful? I don't believe it.'

'Well, it's true. It was an old boyfriend of hers from Darlington – a negro. When he wrote her that he was coming to London I was prepared to welcome him. I said: "We'll show him round London together". But, oh, no, she had to meet him alone, for "Old Time's Sake", she said. Infidelity took place at the Strand Palace Hotel. When I tackled her about it she admitted it – two weeks later. She said it didn't mean anything – but it meant a lot to me.'

Two fat tears fell into the sugar basin and Charley laid his head quietly among the cups.

Eugene was very impressed to hear that the amiable, though rather prosaic Roberta ran off with negroes from Darlington. He thought of her with a new respect.

'Listen, Charley, if she said it didn't mean anything – it didn't. She probably felt sorry for him, being a stranger in London and all and negroes are very attractive. She only did it for old time's sake and she was thinking of you all the time. It didn't mean anything – therefore it didn't happen.'

'It did happen – at the Strand Palace Hotel.' Charley's voice rose bitterly from an ash-tray and a liquorice paper cigarette stuck to his trembling lip.

'You don't know what happened – you weren't there. You're in no position to condemn her, because you are so insufferably smug. No one is in a position to condemn anyone else. The only real crime is not loving enough and therefore you are the guilty one because you don't love Roberta enough to overlook this blunder. She loves you enough to want you to.'

Eugene was beginning to hate Charley more than anyone else in the world, not because he cried, but for his intolerable conceit. His tears were commendable except that he wept for himself needlessly.

'It's no use, Gene. I know you like Roberta, but I am adamant. Surely the last bit of human dignity left to us is the ability to say "I am responsible for my actions".'

'All right,' said Eugene, 'so this one act of kindness to a lonely provincial has cancelled out everything good she did, everything you did together and the fact that she has loved you for six years. You are allowing a Darlington provincial to invalidate six years of your life in one afternoon. You are so criminally stupid that it's no wonder your wife is driven into the arms of other men.'

They jumped to their feet and Eugene landed a blow across the table on Charley's chin, when the café door opened. A rather attractive pig-faced girl of about twenty-four came in and walked towards their table. There was ice on her straight black hair and on the shoulders of her red coat, snow.

Charley pulled out a chair for her.

'Egg and chips, please,' he said to the waiter. Then he took his shoes off and let her warm her feet in them.

'I'm sorry, Roberta,' he said.

Eugene left the café.

He had nothing to do. He 'phoned Abigail, but she was out as he knew she would be, but he let the 'phone ring for five minutes. Spinning four pennies on the telephone stand he remembered the number of a girl he hated called Flo who lived in Ealing.

'Hello, Flo? It's Eugene. I would've been in touch before but I've been in South America for a year. I've had a touch of malaria, too. See you in about half an hour then.' As he spoke he noticed with disgust the phoney phrases that fell from his lips and his insincere diction.

He pulled his waterproof cap down and lit a cigarette and stepped on to the Ealing train. There was no one in his compartment except a woman in white plastic ear-rings reading 'Exodus'. He got out at Ealing Broadway and knocked at the door of Florence's neat bed sitter. It was an action instantly regretted.

'Hi! I'm afraid I've got a frightful cold. Do come in.'

And indeed her nose looked like a scraped carrot and her pale eyes overflowed.

Eugene sat down on the studio couch among hand-sewn scatter cushions. 'I thought we could have something to eat and then go out somewhere this afternoon – perhaps to the zoo.'

'That'd be grand. I'll raid the larder and find us something to eat.'

For a bachelor girl she was a remarkable hog, Eugene thought, as he saw the rows of tins, packets of soup and paper bags destined to become well-balanced meals for one. Florence tied an apron round her pleated waist, rolled the sleeves of her floral blouse up her white arms and set to work, the electric light sparkling on her newly-set hair. Hating her because she was not Abigail whom he loved, Eugene went into the other room and was distressed to hear the sounds of cooking punctuated with sneezing. He contemplated escaping through the third floor window.

The last time he had seen Flo was at her office party two Christmases ago when she had been presented with a certificate for the Oldest Office Junior in Holborn. She mounted the rostrum smilingly to receive her trophy from one of the directors and fell flat on her face.

The other girls accused her of being drunk but she swore with tears in her eyes that she had only had two Babychams and her heel got caught in the hem of her dress. Eugene was asked to leave and later evicted by three members of the firm's cycling club and a lady stenographer in rimless glasses.

He picked up a copy of *Woman* and started to read. There are practically only two stories which appear in various disguises in women's magazines: one is about a country girl who goes to Chelsea and meets a gay artistic bachelor, an interior decorator – they found they shared a passion for Strauss waltzes and Debussy nocturnes – but after a few parties gets jilted and decided she doesn't want to be a sophisticate any more and marries the boy from back home whom she jilted to come to London and sees from the window of the boutique where she works.

The other story is often called 'And Baby Makes Three' and sometimes 'Welcome Stranger'. The young married couple, aged 24 upwards, don't want this baby – their parents told them they were too young to marry and they're beginning to think they may have been right. But when it's born the father sees it's got finger-nails and everything's all right.

The story Eugene read was of the former variety. It contained the most decadent words he had ever read.

The girl had just been jilted and was alone in her Chelsea flat. 'She wasn't hungry but she cooked a well-balanced meal and forced herself to eat it,' and later – 'she felt like crying but decided to have a cup of tea instead.' The most terrible thought was that Flo would not find these two statements decadent.

'Florence,' he shouted, 'what did you do when you got home from the office party? You know you were rather upset?' Again the pseudo 'rather upset'.

Florence stood in the little doorway with a smear of tomato soup on her cheek.

'Well, one or two of the girls were rather beastly to me. They said I'd been pinching the sherry when I knew very well that the Babycham was for the ladies. Then somebody hid my handbag in the cloakroom and they all giggled. When I found it you had disappeared and I had to come home by myself. I felt like having a jolly good cry, but I made myself a nice hot mug of Horlicks and went to bed.'

Mean with her emotions, she was mean with her food. Dinner was tomato soup, fish fingers and pine-apple cubes.

'I never eat much at this time of day,' Flo said, arranging four pineapple cubes in a glass dish.

Eugene looked along the white-painted bookcase. *A Pony for Jill, Jill's Gymkhana, Two Red Rosettes.*

'Have you read *Jill Rides for a Fall?*' asked Eugene. 'Well, this Jill works at the local forge and the day before the Gymkhana all the rich girls from the local riding school bring their ponies to be shod. Jill takes these filthy great nails and drives them right through their shoes into the ground so they can't move. It doesn't hurt them, of course. Anyway, Jill wins the

Gymkhana as she's the only competitor. The judge is just pinning a huge red rosette on her yellow poloneck sweater when hordes of Pony Club members, claws asunder, come charging up on their ponies, whom they have since released. They line up on the ponies in two lines and Jill has to run the gauntlet. Her black velvet cap is poor protection against the evil crops. Her poloneck sweater is slashed with mud. The rosette lies trampled in the mud of the Rectory Field. Then they rip her jodhpurs off—'

Eugene saw his audience was no longer with him – it was putting on a record of 'Vocal Gems from South Pacific'.

'I know you think I'm a bit of a square, but I've had quite a lot of experiences, you know. I was at University.'

'You don't meet real people at University. You've got to go out into the world to meet real people.'

'I was at Durham University.'

They left in silence for the zoo. He lost her on the Mappin Terraces and hid for two hours in the Reptile House.

[13]

The same sluggish morning at 8.10 Abigail, in grey socks, navy-blue mac and carrying a scarlet beret knocked on her friend's door.

Rosemarie's mother in a cotton kimono and rollers in her hair let her in and she stood in the green passage counting the orange ivy leaves on the wallpaper until Rosemarie came down the stairs. A paperback J. B. Philips' translation of the New Testament fell from her satchel and lay fluttering at the foot of the stairs. A year earlier on her birthday an ex-friend Anne had said, handing her a parcel decked with Christmas Sellotape, 'It isn't much, Rosemarie, but I think you'll like it.' The opened parcel revealed the paperback testament and a tin of Nivea.

Cars with chains on their wheels churned up the black hill sending a spray of dirty slush on to the watchers at the bus stop. In front of Rosemarie and Abigail stood a little girl in a too long brown mac and a brown pancake beret covering her ears and scraping the chopped hair from her forehead. When she turned round they saw that her brown eyes were red-rimmed. She cried at the bus stop every morning. Her big shoes stood uneasily side by side, and her shining leather satchel, obviously bought as an Eleven Plus passing present, and gold initialled, bulged unhappily. Her mother waved to her from a lace curtained window across the road and turned back to her housework, having sent her child, crying and in ludicrous apparel, to a day in hell.

They had waited ten minutes. Abigail felt sick with the cold and her leathery breakfast and the brown miserable child.

'I'm not going,' she said.

'Neither am I. Where shall we go?'

'To your place. When does your mother leave?'

'About quarter past nine. We'll have to walk round till then. We have two alternatives, equally foul. If we go up St John's Road we'll have to pass the Stop Children Crossing lady, and if we go down we have to walk past the Launderette.'

They decided to walk down the hill, past the mocking launderette ladies in pink overalls who, interchangeable with their machines, stood at the window, while whiter than bagwash still fell the snow.

The streets were grey and forsaken as they walked past rows of cold houses, empty because their owners, under the impression that to live one must work, were sitting in snow-bound trains reading over each other's shoulders the *Daily Telegraph* and *Woman's Own*.

Abigail said: 'The ultimate degradation is when you see people hurl themselves at the closing doors of the Underground in order to be five minutes earlier for work. It's so terrible when they try and fail, they step back on the platform and self-consciously walk away, I can't look.'

At the end of the road they saw a bright fire burning in a brazier. As they approached Rosemarie recognized the two workmen breaking up the road.

'It's Jim and Tom. They used to work down our road.'

Jim was fair with a foxy Kirk Douglas face and Tom was small with brown spiky hair. His boots made his legs look like Rupert Bear's. They both wore blue jeans and black jackets with leather shoulders. They let the girls sit in their canvas hut while they worked outside. The blue steel picks flashed and bits of broken stone flew. The burning coke and a blackened kettle gave promise of hot sweet tea with condensed milk and carbon monoxide smoke hung in blue rings outside the hut door, thawing and mellowing.

After a bit Jim came in and sat with them, his boots smoking on the brazier, as lumps of snow fell into the flames. He took out his wallet.

'That's my girl friend,' presenting a photograph of a limp girl with scrambled egg hair, flabby shorts and a sun top. 'She's nice, isn't she,' bleated Rosemarie.

'It was taken last year at Butlin's, Skegness.'

A sudden burst of wind lifted the photograph from Jim's hand. For a second it lay on a blue wreath above the fire then fell into the flames, shrivelled and died. They left Jim holding a blackened leg in charred shorts.

It was by now about half past nine and they went to Abigail's place where she changed into jeans and a dirty white mac and packed her uniform into her duffel bag, and thence to Rosemarie's house.

Rosemarie's Nan was on her bird-bone knees sweeping the stairs. She waved the polythene dustpan in a military greeting, a stroke having deprived her of speech two years before. While Rosemarie changed, Abigail made some toast. From the kitchen she could see Rosemarie's cat eating a bird in the snow. She spread the toast with yellow piccalilli and made three cups of Nescafé. They drank it in the front room – Nan had hers on the stairs, but to Abigail it tasted of bird's blood.

Rosemarie begged five shillings from Nan, who snuffled into her apron as she handed it over, and they caught a train to Charing Cross. Wardour Street, Rupert Street and Shaftesbury Avenue, Frith Street, Brewer Street, Wardour Street again, Old Compton Street, Dean Street and Charing Cross Road.

'I wonder what they're doing now?'

'Scripture.'

For a moment there was silence as each heart took its own path and stood for a moment in the cold classroom, hearing the familiar words:

'Rosemarie, take your Bible and go to the back of the class!' The class consisted of people who referred constantly to "Our Lord' and wrote Thee and Thy and Him and His with a capital H and T.

Abigail and Rosemarie looked at each other and laughed. They were back in Frith Street, drifting, when they saw three women. The central one wore a white trenchcoat and hamburger legs terminating in beetle-crusher shoes. The other two had short curly hair and hook noses. One of them carried a tartan shopping bag and an apron peeped from the other's coat.

'Housewife Lesbians,' said Rosemarie. 'The big one's King of all the Lesbians. She presides at their orgies and has several concubines. They call her Big Daddy.'

They followed for a bit and stopped a few inches away and looked into a delicatessen window, while their quarry stood on a corner saying farewell. Big Daddy was telling a story of how she did a ton on the M1 with actions. The housewives shook their heads at her daring. Big Daddy strode in Freddy's Peeperama and was lost and the housewives paddled away through the snow in plastic boots.

'Of course,' said Abigail as they sat drinking coffee in a snack bar, 'I'm not mocking them because they're only people who are a bit different from most people in some ways.'

'Yes.'

Abigail had this terrible experience last summer. She remembered watching the revolving coffee. It was hot and they were drawing in spilled salt on the table. It was so hot that August day that they stayed in the dark of the house, sitting at the table and drawing in spilt salt among the dirty dishes. It was one of those days when the sea is beyond every hill and the dry garden was full of grasshoppers.

Lew came to call for her because they were going out. He was wearing a white shirt which looked good against his dark face, and jeans. The shimmering summer road was bright with hot tar and a cat lay poured across the pavement, hazy rainbows glittering in its dusty fur. They had ten minutes to wait for a train. A woman at the other end of the platform wore a nylon blouse and sagging summer skirt. In summer old women appear in sad floral skirts.

They had the compartment to themselves. Few people entered or left the train at the first four stations, but at London Bridge a woman got in. She had very short white hair lined with pinkish scalp, and sat down in a corner, crossing her thin and freckled but somehow floppy legs. Her long feet wore custard-yellow ankle socks and weather-beating shoes. She began to read and they saw that it was a prayer-book and began to laugh moderately then helplessly, Abigail aware of her stupid laughing face.

When she looked up they saw that she had been reading the Marriage Service. She got out at Waterloo and they saw her get into another compartment further up. Her old cropped head shone white and lonely in the bright sun and Abigail wanted to run after her and tell her how she liked her socks and how she admired the prayer-book, but the train started and they had spoiled someone's summer day. She started crying.

'What the hell's the matter?' Lew said. 'I thought you liked mocking people.'

They found they couldn't pay for the coffee and fled the café and ended up in a News Theatre with two Greek boys.

[14]

More fair than all the Vernal flowers
Embosomed in the dales,
St Winifrede in beauty bloom'd,
The rose of ancient Wales.

With every loveliest grace adorned,
The Lamb's unsullied bride,
Apart from all the world she dwelt
Upon the mountain side.

Caradoc then with impious love,
Her fleeting steps pursued,
And in her sacred maiden blood
His cruel hands imbrued.

He straight the debt of vengeance paid,
Ingulf'd in yawning flame;
But God a deed of wonder wrought
To her immortal fame.

For where the grassy sward received
The martyr's severed head,
This holy fountain upward gush'd
Of crystal vein'd with red.

Here miracles of might are wrought,
Here all diseases fly,
Here see the blind, and speak the dumb,
Who but in faith draw nigh.

Assist us, glorious Winifrede,
Dear Virgin, ever blest!
The passions of our hearts appease
And lull our souls to rest.

The shears of the Barber Nun clicked in rhythm with her song, and a naked head proclaimed another novice.

'What is your name?' asked the Barber Nun.

'I am to be called Sister Winifrede,' answered the novice in sweet tones.

'Indeed!' and so saying she took her shears and sliced the shining head from the kneeling girl's shoulders. Where it fell sprang no miraculous fount, only a bitter briar sprang up with thorns.

The Barber Nun picked up the severed head and carried it to the refectory where Sister Mary Joseph was preparing the feast for the evening banquet. It was celebration night at the Our Lady of the Sorrows' Convent for it was the Mother Superior's birthday. Sister Mary Joseph finished pulling cooked legs off a hen and took Sister Winifrede's head and broiled it with saxifrage and feverfew. When it was done she garnished it with rich brown sauce and set flowers in the hair and garlanded the head and set it on a golden platter. Swine fever having ransacked the convent sties and carried off several of the sisters, Sister Mary Joseph regarded Sister Winifrede as, like the ram caught in the thicket, a timely gift from the Almighty, a substitute for the traditional boar's head.

It so happened that the Mother Superior had sent out into the highways and byways of the adjacent village and brought in poor, the maimed and the lame to share her feast. Serene and smiling sisters plied the old folks with goodies.

When the feast was eaten the Barber Nun proposed a short service of thanksgiving for the supreme gift of Sister Winifrede, and the Mother Superior led a conga of the sisters, the blind, the dumb, the maimed and the lame snaking through the tombstones to the blood-red briar. The body of Sister Winifrede was not to be found but two gardener nuns giggled conspicuously in front of the compost heap.

'Sisters, Ladies, Gentlemen, the Deformed,' began the Mother Superior, 'we are gathered together at the shrine of Sister Winifrede to celebrate her miraculous conversion and subsequent death. Let us remember for a moment, her namesake, Saint Winifrede, the flower of Wales.' Her clear voice rose in a silver stream and hung, a trembling alto castrato, above the heads of the kneeling crowd.

> 'Here miracles of might are wrought
> Here all diseases fly,
> Here see the blind, and speak the dumb,
> Who but in faith draw nigh.'

'To us in the Our Lady of the Sorrows' Convent has been granted a similar miracle. Behold! The blood-red briar which has sprung from the precious life blood of Sister Winifrede. I want two volunteers, one maimed and one dumb.'

Eager nuns pushed two figures into a kneeling position before the Mother Superior. One carried a small crutch and the other looked normal save for a black patch over his mouth.

Gently the Mother Superior broke off two leaves from the briar and gave one to each of the supplicants. The dumb man raised the patch from his panting lips and bit deeply into the dark red leaf. A low moan broke from the lips of the watchers. He cast away the black patch from his mouth, opened his lips, and spoke: 'Holy Mother . . .' he began, then his face turned the colour of blood and he went leaping over the gravestones blaspheming and barking like a dog.

The Mother Superior turned to the maimed man who had kept silent. He lay paralysed upon the cold ground at her feet, his feet pointing towards the moon and his head to the grave. His crutch crossed itself and hopped away, click click on the tombstones into the dark.

> 'Assist us, Glorious Winifrede,
> Dear Virgin! Ever blest!
> The passions of our hearts appease
> And lull our souls to rest.'

[15]

They came out of the theatre, Abigail and Eugene, running, their feet pounding on the packed ice of the car park and into a black Chevrolet, the brakes grinding as the car leaped into the crowded road. The shouts behind them burst in the cold neon sky and green and yellow lights died on cold faces alongside. Then across London Bridge, astride the black running river and pale masts and misty strings of lamps spinning past and the whole world turning and the car leaping towards the edge of the world.

Ice thickened on the windscreen and Eugene looked out through a narrow clear arc at the speeding Old Kent Road, the short fur bristling on his arms and on the backs of his capable mole hands, on into the night of South East London.

The Chevrolet skimmed the shrieking pavement edge and roared backwards on two wheels in a shower of glass through a traffic island and into the face of an oncoming bubble car.

Eugene lay on the road masked in blood; he saw a deflated bubble car and the white ground revolving upwards with the approaching sirens to the cold stars of New Cross, and in the black wreck a girl screaming.

Eugene was walking along a wide empty road in deep snow. Soft snowflakes like birds filled the sky and floating slowly among the snowflakes were angels with white trumpets and holding white flags. The sky was full of angels. He plucked an angel from the sky and took her to a sordid tenement.

He woke up between the cold utility sheets of the prison hospital.

[16]

As she walked into the Female Prisoners' Waiting Room two weeks later, Abigail saw that somebody had scratched 'BASTARDS' on the door. Her mother followed, tight lipped, and sat on one of the benches which ran round the edge of the grey room. Abigail sat down too at some distance.

Adjoining the Female Prisoners' Waiting Room was a lavatory. From time to time they heard a flushing sound, then a woman with grey hair and red lipstick came into the room. She was about sixty and so were her hips, and she wore a black dress with a heavy chain hanging out of her pocket, which she fingered all the time. She had a list and called out people's names. She called out 'Annabel Fawkes' instead of Abigail. When she came to the name 'Thompson' she opened the lavatory door and stuck her head in and shouted:

'Are you all right, Thompson? How long are you going to be in there?'

There was a Jewish prostitute called Rabinowitz who told Abigail that she had just gone out from the club where she worked to get an ice-cream when she was charged with obstruction. She was with an Irish girl called Rita Monahan.

Then the grey-haired woman departed. Abigail heard a constable address her as 'Matron'.

The woman called Thompson came out of the lavatory. She was short with short straight black hair and a child's navy-blue gabardine, too short, revealing Mongol legs in lisle stockings and black plimsolls. She went out into the corridor and asked for a cigarette. A policeman obviously gave her one because she came back with a lighted cigarette between her lips. A moment later she opened the door again and threw it out and screamed, 'I didn't ask for a bloody filter tip.'

They had taken her bag away from her and she opened the door again and shouted: 'Why can't I have my bag? They've all got their bags,' and pointed to the others on the benches.

'We thought you might bash the magistrate over the head with it,' laughed a young policeman, and he closed the door.

Thompson opened the door and he closed it. She opened it again and he swore and crashed it shut in her face. She went back into the lavatory and shut the door behind her.

Rabinowitz and Rita Monahan were called and they walked out smiling.

Abigail felt sorry for her mother being in such surroundings; she pressed her hand by way of encouragement, but Mrs Fawkes sniffed and withdrew her hand.

When she stood in the dock everything became blurred. She saw the magistrate dressed in black at a desk and other people in black sitting at a table. Then Eugene was put beside her with a bandaged head. She felt him take her fingers under the rim of the dock and play with them. She didn't listen to what they were saying. Across the court she could see Matron and she fixed her eyes upon her, counting silver buttons and the links in her thick chain, seven silver buttons, eleven links, then the obscuring pocket, two steel eyes, one merged red lip, hair shaved at the sides, two black laced-up feet with legs growing out of them, seven buttons, eleven steel links, two fat hands, one cruel nose.

She heard the magistrate propose to make an example of someone, then she realized it was Eugene. He was sentenced to two years' imprisonment for stealing the car and dangerous driving and deflating the bubble car, the owner of which escaped with minor abrasions. Abigail was conditionally discharged on account of her age and she felt humbled and ashamed when Eugene was led away in bandages by two policemen.

She looked down at her hands resting quietly on the edge of the dock like a dead bird's claws and saw that he had slipped his ring on to her finger.

Matron led her out and at the door she said: 'I hope you've learned your lesson.'

'I'm sure she has,' said Mrs Fawkes.

They went home in silence. Her mother was ostracizing her completely and the hard sun made her cut leg ache. In the afternoon she lay on her bed reading, and in the evening after her mother had gone to bed she lay on the floor listening to Radio Luxembourg.

Abigail woke suddenly and cried out in loneliness. The light was still on but the wireless was dead. Her shoes were on the wrong feet and it was the loneliest moment of her life. She went into her mother's bedroom and Mrs Fawkes quickly pulled the covers over her face and turned to the wall. 'Mum . . .' said Abigail. 'Please . . .' There was no answer only the simulated regular breathing beneath the candlewick bedspread. 'All right, you bitch, I am not going to beg for your conversation because I don't want it anyway,' she said and went downstairs where she fell on the floor and cried for an hour, clawing her face with Eugene's ring until bitter red scratches stood out on her face, inflamed with the salt of her tears.

Then she sat up. She felt wide awake and dead inside, so she opened a packet of cigarettes and, lighting them, stood them upright round the room.

In the morning there were little broken pillars of ash in rows on the table and on the arms of chairs and they stood in a drunken platoon on the windowledge until a robin flew down and brushed them into the sad blue sky with his soft wings.

[17]

Davis walked in the cold spiritual blue morning up the steps and knocked on Mrs Mayhew's door.

She opened it, a tape measure in one hand and in the other a tin of Nescafé.

'Why, Mr Davis! Come on in. I was just measuring the Nescafé – these Indians have been at it again.' Davis took off his Pakamac and matching cap and sat down in a kitchen chair. A shiny new hearing aid gleamed on his chest.

The room was very warm and his shoes began to steam. Mrs Mayhew opened a tin of oxtail soup and cut some bread and they ate it at the formica kitchen table.

Davis felt welcome and secure. He took off his shoes and rubbed his thick woollen feet against Mrs Mayhew's legs, up and down. She pretended not to notice – blowing and dipping her bread in the soup. Then she giggled and choked but she did not remove her legs.

He took her by the arm and led her into the bedroom. She sat laughing on the bed with her legs sticking out like rhubarb in front of her and Davis pulled off her slippers savagely and then her hairnet. She saw her face, a white blur in the mirror and her mushroom-coloured hair fell softly about her shoulders. Then she went slowly smiling into David's thin arms like a young and beautiful girl.

Afterwards she covered them both up with the sheet

and they lay side by side in the cool world. Davis let his foot slide down the sheet into the frozen antarctic regions and drew it up deliciously. Mrs Mayhew stroked his thin grey hair and traced the bones of his sweaty face.

'Mrs Mayhew, it is very wonderful to find a woman who is a woman. Now that we have found each other at last we must waste no time.'

They dressed and he helped her on with her nylon fur coat and she put a polythene headscarf in the handbag in case of rain.

'Here, let me do that, dear,' and she adjusted the flex of his hearing aid.

They walked out into the February afternoon. The sun sparkled on the frosty pavements and the trees were black against the powder-blue sky and stamping bright staccato feet, the bugling birds filled the roofs and hedges of Victoria.

Mrs Mayhew's feet beat a happy tattoo on the empty pavement – 'Once you have caught him never let him go. Once you have caught him never let him go,' her spiked heels sang and she held Davis's arm tight and proudly.

They got on a bus and got off at Hampstead. Davis guided her into a pub and ordered a brown ale and a bitter lemon and some cheese sandwiches. Then they wandered hand in hand to Hampstead Heath. After walking for about fifteen minutes they sat on a bench and Davis took from his neck a holy medallion, placed there by Sister Mary Magdalene Kavanagh once after Vespers in the stillness of the cloisters, and fastened it round Mrs Mayhew's neck.

They walked on until, standing on top of a hill, they

saw in a hollow below them roundabouts and stalls and swings. The sun caught the gilt and chrome so that the fairground was on fire with light and the shouting people moved like angels with faces aflame.

It began to get dark as they hurried down to the fair and rain spattered in the hot dog grease. They climbed on to the great whistling horses of the roundabout and as the horses began rearing and plunging the organ pipes and drums at the centre played: 'When you are in love it's the loveliest night of the year', and they galloped faster and faster until the painted clowns and cherubs, pink roses and gilt mirrors were one with the horses, spinning out into the darkness among the stars.

Davis and Mrs Mayhew staggered off their tired horses and into the blinding rain. Thunder was coming closer and they stood for shelter under the bingo stall. She hid her face in his shoulder as the approaching lightning sparked in the wet black sky. Soon most of the crowd had dispersed.

'Let's just go on the bumper cars, then we'll go home,' said Mrs Mayhew.

They chose a yellow car with Thunderbird painted on the side in black. Mrs Mayhew took the wheel. They were the only occupants of the cars but the boy took their money and started the car. She drove twice round the rink, skilfully negotiating the stationary red and green vehicles huddled at the edge of the track.

A sudden terrific burst of thunder crashed above their heads and fire flashed along the cables and for a second every car was a hot agony of twisted metal.

Mrs Mayhew's long scream projected into the blue

flares and was broken by melted steel. Chunks of burning wood fell about their blackened mouths as the blistered car drifted lazily backwards along the red-hot grid.

18

Eugene sat on his bunk warming his hands on his tin mug of cocoa. He wished he was dead. Abigail had not been allowed to visit him, he did not know where she was or who she was with. He lay down and pulled the grey blanket over his face and lay awake all night.

The next day at dinner an Indian boy, a newcomer, sat beside him, and suddenly dropped his head down on the wooden table and cried. The men mocked him and a bald-headed man with pebble glasses stole his soup. The boy was put in the same cell as Eugene who tried to talk to him but he sat with his head on his knees rocking backwards and sideways in silence.

As if regretting his public grief the boy quietly hanged himself in the night in a sheet hung from the window. When they cut him down in the morning Eugene found a crumpled photograph of a lovely Indian girl on the floor and he put it in the boy's pocket.

What Eugene hated most was his trousers. He was used to wearing narrow slim corduroy trousers and these were shapeless, baggy and too short and made his legs look deformed. After two weeks he tore them on a nail in the bed and was given another pair. He put his hands in his pockets and drew out a photograph. He knew he was wearing the trousers of the dead Indian boy.

He was ashamed of his hands. They were pricked by needles and rough with sewing. His nails were grimed and his thin fingers shook when he tried to thread his needle. His hair had been cut very short. Abigail's letters he wore inside his shirt and his finger felt naked without his ring.

19

So Abigail was alone in the shrunken green summer. She walked through the hot London streets, through the twisting smiling crowds, with her eyes half closed against the sun and the laughter of which she was no part. And all the time she was thinking, if I do not see him, if he has stopped loving me, I shall die.

The world was deformed and pornographic. She opened her eyes upon the wheels of wheelchairs shining in the dusty sun and crutches and burnt faces and eyeless faces and faces without noses. Old women in white ankle socks and men in cardigans and moustaches and children in broken glasses crowded the holiday streets, their ice-cream faces melting as August exploded in the hot sky.

And in the long summer nights she would stand in the dark garden with the long wet grass on her legs among the white roses, and then it was worst of all because the night was so beautiful and she stood alone under the black sky filled with white stars.

One night when she was walking home from the pictures with her friend Jane she looked round her at the high buildings in the driving rain. The husky lips of straws and paper mouths of bags sucked the black drops in the gutter and little bitter streams intersected the pavement dust. She thought: 'If I look up I will see a sign.' She looked up, but there was no great gold Jesus in the sky saying with open arms:

> 'Art thou weary? Art thou languid?
> Are thou sore distrest?
> Come to me, saith one, and coming
> Be at rest.'

Only a transistor crying in the empty sky.

Then one night when she went out late to post a letter the sky was low with thick white mist although it was only August, and there was a bonfire smell in the air. Soon leaves turned yellow and fell, choking the gutters and rain gurgled in the drains. The sky became very blue in the daytime, so blue it seemed that it would crack.

She was living on a little island doing only necessary tasks, surrounded by an ocean of desolation. 'God is dead,' she thought, 'and the world is hurling towards destruction.'

She had a dream in September which was unutterably depressing. Eugene had just been released and they were at a big celebration party. Eugene was organizing a game, he shouted something in French, then everyone repeated it, dodging in and out of white stone alcoves. She went and pulled him by the sleeve and said, 'I want to talk to you.' They left the party and went into a bathroom. 'You've stopped loving me, haven't you?' she said. Eugene just turned his face to the wall and said, 'I'm sorry.'

In the morning when she awoke she was sure he didn't love her any more. Instead of sending him her usual letter she sent him a card for Yom Kippur.

His letters said he still loved her. The sad curtains that oppressed her window depressed her, she thought that even the cat rejected her. Then came the yearly

Christmas crucifixion in the butchers' shops and she watched her mother eat a goose laughing with her friends.

It was the first time she saw him after the crash because permitted visits were infrequent. There was a grille between them like a confessional. Humbled by the presence of a warder, Eugene was the applicant for absolution. She stared at his clenched quiet hands pricked with needles in the sewing shop. It was not the dead look in his eyes, it was the humiliation of his hands that was hardest to bear. She said:

'Do you still love me?'

'Yes.'

'Are you sure?'

'I have never stopped loving you for one moment and I never will.'

'Prove it to me. It is so terrible without you. I've got to have proof that you love me. If you do, escape from here.'

The warder's eyes doubled vigilance.

'We'll go away somewhere. We'll go to San Marino. Please, Eugene. If you really love me you will.'

'I'll prove it in a better way – I'll design a cathedral for you.' The brown and cream walls closed in on her.

'No. No. You've got to prove it my way or it isn't proof. I don't want a cathedral – I want you. You are letting these people turn you into a sheep.'

'Time's up,' said the warder, and a lady officer escorted her out.

[20]

On Wednesday the fourth of January fire broke out in the prison. All but one man were quickly marshalled to safety. Eugene was hit by a falling beam. He was not killed trying to save the crippled forger who shared his cell. He was killed trying to escape.

[21]

'Well, it's time you did something useful. You don't go to school, you don't go to work. You just lie on your bed all day doing nothing. Why don't you learn short-hand and typing and get yourself a good job?'

Eugene was in a far off hell and she was here. Around her forever stretched the black eternity. The howling and beating of fists had achieved nothing, neither would this.

'Yes,' she said, 'I will learn shorthand and typing,' because she knew she was already dead.

THE END

Shena Mackay

TODDLER ON THE RUN

Toddler on The Run

[1]

Morris opened his eyes upon the yellow sky and his ears to the screaming of birds. He went, trailing wet willowherb, to the narrow path and walked discreetly between the nettles because they were taller than he. Morris Todd was twenty-three and three feet nine tall.

Elaine was hanging out the washing in the garden when she turned and saw his sweet corrupt face through the mimosa. They walked through the wet grass into the house.

'You haven't met the new addition to the family, have you?'

'Not a baby?'

'Certainly not. Come and meet him.'

A black Chow lifted his diamante head from the water-bowl and laid it at Elaine's feet. Morris watched her white fingers stroke his triangular ears. Then they went upstairs and Elaine turned on the taps in the bathroom and left him.

'I can't say I'm terribly thrilled to see him again,' said Daniel. 'There is a certain ambivalence in my attitude to dwarfs. There's something not quite nice about him.'

'It's only his mind that's warped, he's got a lovely little body.'

Upstairs Morris sang as he dressed. He slicked back his black hair and went down.

'Tartan trews!' said Elaine.

1

'I got them off a clothes line. My others are ruined. Like them?'

'Fabulous,' said Daniel and left the room.

'O Morris, you haven't been stealing again, have you?' asked Elaine although she knew he had.

She watched him eating a fried egg. He cut off and ate the white in strips and put the rest whole into his mouth because he could not bear the violation of the golden yolk.

'I suppose you're in some kind of trouble.'

'Yes,' and while he demolished five cups of tea and five pieces of toast, Morris who sometimes had the manners of a pig, told her the reason for his flight to Kent.

[2]

Leda had sat in the Deptford Odeon and watched Morris standing smaller than the others in the queue for ices and peanuts in his leather jacket.

After the film they met a friend of Morris, Tom, in the foyer.

'I didn't see you inside,' he said.

'We always sit upstairs,' said Leda.

'I've got something to tell you,' Tom said to Morris. 'When can I talk to you?'

'See you here in ten minutes.'

Morris took Leda to the bus stop and watched her disappear into the wilderness of New Cross. Tom waved to him from the 'Peace then Plenty' coffee stall, since demolished and replaced by a public convenience. They were alone except for a tramp whose tired eyes slept in a pool of cold tea.

But he never knew what Tom had to tell him. The proprietor looked at Tom and said, 'You're Tom Loveday, aren't you?'

'Why?'

'Sod off.'

'Kindly elucidate,' said Morris.

'The police have been here and I think they're looking for you. I don't want them to find you here when they come back. This is a respectable stall and I don't want my name in the *Kentish Mercury*.'

'Where can we go?' said Tom, pulling the nylon fur

3

collar of his coat round his neck as they stood abandoned in the rain.

'Manny's place. They won't look for us there.'

Lame Manny Margolis took them in. He took a *Kentish Mercury* from an occasional table and showed it to them.

TODDLER WANTED FOR THEFT

Greenwich CID are anxious to question a man and a boy aged about three in connection with the theft . . .

'Three!' said Morris.

'I knocked off his glasses, remember?'

. . . of £923 2s 7d from St Alfege's school last Tuesday. The man helped himself to the cash while the boy, wearing a leather jacket, menaced the school caretaker with a gun. The money was raised by the girls of St Alfege's towards the building of a new swimming pool. Mr George Ambrose, the caretaker, described his assailants as being one of them a tall greasy chap and the other an evil sort of toddler. 'It was a big gun,' he said, 'and he had to use both hands.' The headmistress, Miss L. Lambe, commented, 'It was a mean trick. I appeal personally to the thieves to return the money and face the consequences of their actions.'

While they were laughing Gloria Margolis came from the bathroom with tendrils of steam still curling round her face.

'You'll have to go,' she said, the pores opening and closing on her thick face and her big lips purple against her electric-blue housecoat. 'There's no room for you here. I don't want Manny mixed up in anything criminal. It's a diabolical liberty coming here in the first place.'

'Now, Gloria,' said Manny, 'I wouldn't turn a dog out on a night like this.'

'Neither would I.'

'I know a place you can hide,' said Manny. 'It's at the back of UGB. I'll take you there.'

They had to crawl single file along the top at the United Glass Bottles Company's wall.

'It's a bit dodgy,' Manny told them. 'You have to avoid the bits of broken glass. Just keep your fingers crossed and trust in the Almighty— AAAOOOOOOO.

There was an appalling crash and death came at the end for Manny Margolis.

Morris and Tom clung to the sharp wall with their fingers and knees as the sound of broken glass rang and crashed in their ears and the terrible scream shrieked and shrieked cutting up the quiet night as if with broken bottles.

'I'll call an ambulance,' said Tom and he jumped into the road and ran into the blackness. If Morris had shaken the thick tears from his eyes he might have seen Tom hail a passing taxi and ride out of his life.

He sat rigid on the wall waiting for the night to be filled with running feet and cries and police whistles but none came and he listened to the rain drumming on the broken bottles below and thought how cold it must be down there. 'Here's my coat, Manny,' and he took it off and threw it down. After half an hour's silent wake on the wall he was so cold that he couldn't grip the wet bricks any longer and dropped down to the pavement and walked with stinging ankles to a 'phone box and ordered an ambulance. Then he went back to Charlton Church Lane and put £100 in notes, which he had had concealed about his person, through Gloria Margolis's letter box.

The following day the papers proclaimed 'DEATH FALL. POLICE SEEK TODDLER.' The schoolkeeper had identified his jacket. Meanwhile Morris was aboard a Kent-bound train and Leda Teagarden searched in vain the dripping streets of SE London.

[3]

At teatime Daniel said: 'This is a delicious salad, darling. Incidentally, I wish that dog would take his meals from the floor like a normal animal.'

The dog helped himself to a slice of cucumber with his discriminating snout.

'I have an interesting theory,' said Morris, looking at Daniel. 'It is that the person who takes the second last slice of bread is morally guiltier than the one who takes the last slice because he has deliberately hurried in order to grab the second last slice, thus making the genuinely hungry person who takes the last slice appear mean and grasping in the eyes of the assembled company.'

Morris destroyed a piece of fruit cake with his delicate hands; he ate only the cherries and left the carnage of ruined raisins and crumbs about his plate. Then his hand flickered towards the Swiss roll and was chastened by a low remark from Daniel.

'O Daniel, you're not being horrible again, are you?' said Elaine, hiding a greenfly with her knife.

'If being horrible constitutes pointing out the fact that he will be the only person to have two pieces of Swiss roll, then I must plead guilty.'

After tea Daniel was stacking the plates on the draining board when he looked down and saw Scott, the Chow, watching him, his black tongue pearled with drops of milk. Daniel seized an apron hanging on the door and tied it round the dog and was plunging his paws into the soapy water when Elaine came in carrying the cups, which she dropped, and seized Scott from his arms and wrenched off the apron.

'How dare you humiliate my dog!'

'After all it's only fair,' Daniel remonstrated laughingly. 'Those who don't work don't eat,' but Elaine flung out of the room and he was left crouching to gather up the broken pieces into the apron.

Later the laughter of Morris and Elaine making the spare bed drifted downstairs and dissolved bitterly in Daniel's lonely brandy glass.

'Morris!' he shouted, 'Morris!' and when he appeared in the doorway poured himself another glass of brandy.

'Cheers,' he said and then, 'You must realize my position, Todd. If I am found harbouring a criminal I'm ruined – an object of derision in Lincoln's Inn Fields. Loath as I am to offend one of Elaine's old friends, I must ask you to leave immediately and via the back door. Please don't attempt to communicate with Elaine. If there is anything I can do in my professional capacity . . .'

'Very well, Daniel. My regards to your esteemed wife. I shall think of you as I lie beneath the stars at peace with nature and my God.'

Daniel recalled these words as he watched him climb through the fence and skip into the dust at peace neither with himself nor God.

Later when tidying up in tears Elaine found a button in one of the glasses which she believed Morris had left as a sign. Her elbow slipped and as pieces of lustre fell about her feet, 'Ah, oh, the Sunderland Loving Cup,' she moaned.

[4]

When he thought he was out of sight Morris relaxed his happy hopping into a gait of despair. He made his way to the station and waited on the platform which hung like a fortress among an invasion of green and copper beeches.

As the Charing Cross train pulled out of the station a chalk-blue butterfly drifted across the window leaving a bleary trail in the dust.

The following morning a girl unknown to Morris was walking along Trafalgar Road, Greenwich. She caught a glimpse of her reflection in a dry cleaners' window and made a mental note to commit suicide. She was D. K. McGovern, Vice-Games Captain of St Alfege's Girls' School, and she walked in desolation to Greenwich Park although it was Monday and games first lesson.

A sad story is attached to the name of D. K. McGovern, for on the previous Saturday at the age of 17·25 years her youth had ended.

Since the day she had been picked for the House Under 13 Hockey team sport had been her life and she had climbed a ladder of hockey sticks to popularity and success. The morning for which she had been created dawned. Her white shorts sparkling and her life blood bouncing in the rubber studs of her boots she strode into position in the match against Ranelagh House School, watched by the England Selectors.

'TWO FOUR SIX EIGHT
Who do we appreciate?
D E I R D R E
Deirdre!'

shouted three juniors who had a crush on her, holding
their blue berets against the wind. It had been a grand
game and as she and Jill ambled off the field she suddenly realized what Miss Lambe meant when she said
every morning:

' . . . To fight and not to heed the wounds . . .'

and looked down and smiled upon her bruised shin.

But as they passed the staff cloakroom the door was
ajar and above the splashing shower they heard:

'Frankly, Miss Baker, she's erratic. And in a centre-
forward that's fatal . . .'

'She didn't say centre-forward, did she? She didn't,
did she?' begged D. K. McGovern.

'I don't think so – thought she said centre-half,' said
Jill but triumph shone in her eyes.

Saturday was also the night of a fund-raising dance to
make up for the loss of the swimming pool money and
the Sixth Form had decorated the hall with paper stars.

'Do I look all right?' whispered Deirdre, for that was
her name and dressed in pink she had resolved to dance
away her sorrows and erase the lost years of stick
practice in the pursuit of love.

'You look fab,' smiled false Jill.

'Not at all – erratic?'

'What? – O look, there's Tony,' and Jill danced across
the floor and disappeared.

Deirdre dabbed her eyes with a Kleenex and heard Miss Lambe say through a megaphone:

'This is supposed to be a dance. If the boys of St Thomas's persist in refusing to ask the girls to dance, everyone will be sent home.'

Deirdre went over to the refreshment stall where Miss Baker presided.

'Want any help with the orange squash, Miss Baker?'

'No thanks, D.K. – you run along and enjoy yourself. Bad luck about the match!'

Deirdre moved away. Almost everyone was dancing now. She stood by the record player and looked down upon the pink accordion pleats and wished she was dead. She was spoken to only by girls. The years of team spirit had taken their toll – her face was weatherbeaten, her hands as clumsy as rounder-bats and her calf muscles bulged and shone under the strained stockings. She went into the cloakroom and cried – alone with her ruined legs.

She lay on the grass in Greenwich Park watching a dog barking at a squirrel. It jumped on thin frantic legs under the tree, barking itself hoarse, then suddenly it stopped and started sniffing at a bundle of wet clothes lying in a hollow near the path. The bundle sat up in fear and jumped away from the dog and started running in Deirdre's direction, it seemed to be a little boy and Deirdre ran to pick him up. The dog ran away.

'You poor little thing,' said Deirdre. 'Where's your mummy? – ouch!' and she quickly dropped him in receipt of a vicious blow. Morris sat up and for ten minutes endeavoured to explain that he was not a lost child.

'Don't be so silly,' said Deirdre. 'You'd better tell

11

me where you live or I'll take you to a keeper. It's disgraceful that you should be allowed out alone. Come along,' and she grabbed his wrist.

'Why I should waste my time talking to an over-grown schoolgirl, I don't know. At your age you should know better than to wear that appalling uniform – you look hideous in that beret. Take it off immediately.'

Her fingers faltered and he pulled his hand away. When he had walked a few yards he turned round and saw her lying sobbing in the grass and forced himself to retrace his steps. He put his arm round her shoulders and tried to pull her head up.

'Ah, poor little girl,' he said drying her tears on a handful of grass. 'Don't cry, you're spoiling your lovely eyes. That's better. What school do you go to? St Alfege's? Isn't that where they have the marvellous swimming facilities?'

'I hate them! I hate their beastly swimming pool fund. I'm glad the money was stolen!'

'Really? Well, if you're a good girl and stop crying I'll let you into a little secret and then we'll go and buy you some nice clothes and you can throw away that revolting uniform for ever.'

Half an hour later the curtain of a changing room in Chessman's of Lewisham opened.

'Who is this vision in the cerise négligée?'

'I just wanted to show it to you – I'm wearing the slacks now.'

'Please keep it on – you look so ravishing.'

'O – ooh.'

She reappeared in slacks and suède jacket.

'How can I explain these clothes to Mummy and

Daddy?' asked Deirdre as she sipped a hot chocolate in the Wimpy.

'What do you mean? You're not going home. You're coming with me, remember?'

'I want to go home. You can keep your old clothes. I'm going and you can't stop me – you're only a dwarf.'

Morris was already regretting his impulse of friendship to this lump of tears and muscle and apparently she regretted her rash greed for finery. However, he thought that he could not afford to leave her now with the clothes and knowledge of his identity which she would doubtless gladly impart to the police, and he decided to place her temporarily in a place of safety while he decided what to do with her.

'If you go to the police, you'll be in trouble too. Receiving – let's see, that's two years' probation and your name in the *Mercury*. I may be a dwarf but you're nothing – a failed hockey player and social reject. If you go home they'll only send you back to St Alfege's which has made you what you are.

'One Wimpy cheeseburger and a beefburger please.'

'You know what you said in the park? Did you mean it?'

'Probably not.'

'Have I really got nice eyes?'

'Yes.'

'I will come with you then.'

'Right. First of all I have to find a friend of mine who can help us. You can stay with my grandmother till I fetch you. Here's the address. I'll take you to the bus stop. Just say you're a friend of mine and she'll make you welcome.'

Deirdre gave his hand a little squeeze under the table: 'It's exciting, isn't it?'

As they stood at the bus stop rain began to fall.

'Isn't there anything you want to do, Morris?'

'No, I don't think so. What? Oh, I see. Yes, of course.' He kissed the wet face bent towards him.

'Good-bye my erotic little centre-forward,' he murmured.

'Erratic! Good-bye, Morris.'

[5]

Leda Leda Leda screeched the tyres on the wet road and beat the feet of the shoving Deptford shoppers. When he saw the red and blue Underground sign of New Cross Station Morris started running and didn't stop until he reached Amersham Road and leaned panting on the loved blue door. Silence answered the bell again and again. He sat on the step and watched the azaleas dying in the rain. Then through his knees his sunk head saw coming up the road a white bundle bumping against the blurred white legs and rain spurting from the slopping shoes. She sat beside him on the step, her hostile eyes burning him through lashes like wet paint-brushes and ineffectually pulling the tight black skirt over her knees.

'Leda,' he put his hand on her neck under the hot mustard-coloured hair. She didn't answer, only scratched the step with a green comb.

'Been to the Launderette?'

'Does it look like I've been to the Launderette?'

'Yes.'

'Don't ask pointless questions then.'

'Leda' – catching her thin bare arm – 'must you always criticize me? I was so happy to be with you again and you're determined to spoil my pleasure, aren't you?'

'I am not determined to spoil your pleasure. I haven't seen you for nearly a week and you talk about the Launderette.'

15

'I hoped you would be here. Is it your lunch hour?'

'It so happens that I don't go to work.'

'Why not?'

'Mind your own business.'

'Oh, Leda, must we always quarrel?'

'For Christ sake stop sighing.'

'In all my life,' said Morris in a voice soft with self pity, 'no one has ever treated me so badly.'

'About time someone did then. You've been spoiled all your life by your bloody grandmother.'

'My what grandmother?'

'Oh nothing. You know I like your grandmother.'

'Is it absolutely necessary to sit on these steps?'

'No, of course not. Let's go indoors. Come on, Morry – you know I like your grandmother – I even went to see her the other day. She gave me a lovely tea and then we watched television.'

Morris leaned back on the door while her bright hypocritical voice ran on and the sun ignited the rhododendrons next door.

'They showed that Leonardo cartoon and your grandmother said she didn't see the point of it and she couldn't see what he was trying to poke fun at so I said "Jesus" and she said, "There's nothing ludicrous about Our Lord that they should poke fun at him on television." When I told her my mother worked at the biscuit factory she said, "I hear they have blacks working there. It isn't right to let them handle the biscuits that people have to eat." So I said they only handle the chocolate ones and they have Anglo-Indians to make the chocolate wholemeal. What I really wanted to know was where you were but she didn't know and what's more didn't care. Who do you think you're shoving? . . .'

16

The passing policeman saw only a thin girl in a grubby *broderie anglaise* blouse sitting on the steps by a Launderette bag. As the blue legs receded Morris emerged from behind her and they went into the house where the old smell of lino and biscuits hit him in the pit of the stomach. 'Even the apples are polished,' he thought as he took one from the Pyrex bowl.

'Why are you so scared of the Law all of a sudden? Got a guilty conscience? Incidentally,' she said between bites of her apple, 'you'll be sorry to hear that your friend Manny Margolis has passed away.'

'What do you mean, passed away?'

'There's no need to scream at me. Passed away or murdered – it doesn't matter – he's dead anyway. Please remove your hands – I am trying to eat an apple.'

'He wasn't murdered – he fell. It wasn't my fault, Leda, you've got to believe me. I tried to save him. Tom abandoned him when he was dead so if anyone's to blame it's Tom. Manny was like a brother to me.'

'He wasn't.'

'Please, Leda. I don't want to talk about Manny. Every time I see a milk bottle I think of him.'

'Supposing Gloria tells the police you and Tom were there that night?'

'She'll also have to tell them she accepted £100 in receipt of her husband's corpse. I don't really look three, do I?'

'No, you look at least four,' said loyal Leda.

'I shall treat that remark with the contempt it – Leda, come away with me. It's dangerous here. I've got to leave tonight.'

'Nobody's stopping you.'

'I can't go without you, Leda. I love you, Leda. Please come with me.'

'You know I can't.'

'You would if you loved me.'

'Well, I don't.'

Morris's gesturing hand stopped and fell. He walked out of the room and was at the front door, his hand poised to turn the knob when she should appear, when she shouted:

'Where are you going?'

'To the police.'

'They'll arrest you and you'll be hanged and a good job too because society should be rid of pests like you. I think people like you should be drowned at birth or sent to live in special homes away from the rest of the world. On Christmas Island for instance.'

'A man can do only that which he believes to be right. Good-bye, Leda. When the reporters come tell them that the killer dwarf gave himself up because the person he loved more than anything else in this world failed him in his hour of need.'

An hour later they were safely in a Newhaven-bound train. Morris looked across at her sitting looking out of the window, cigarette ash dropping unnoticed on the knee of her tight pink jeans. Above her on the rack her duffel bag. Morris had learned to look at people relatively and when he looked at Leda he saw only a tired little girl setting out on a visit to some unknown hell. He leaned over and brushed the ash from her knee.

'If you want to go back, darling, it's all right with me,' he said, but she didn't answer and the train went on past Gatwick Airport.

By the time they had walked the length of Newhaven

Harbour Station and given in their tickets their jeans were soaked to their legs and their hair dripped in wet strings as they surveyed the grey desolation before them.

[6]

A little dust had gathered in the corners of the yellowed silver frame on the mantelpiece from which Morris smiled between a saucer of hairpins and a green alarm clock lying on its face.

Deirdre shifted on her chair and the heavy photograph album slipped from her fingers and crashed on to her foot. She brushed a tear from her eye with the back of her hand but another fell on to the album. Morris's grandmother leaned over to pluck out a faded press-cutting and Deirdre stared with dread at the great tear glistening on the black paper but it lay unnoticed.

'This is my daughter's wedding. That's me. "The bride's mother wore a *crème de menthe* wool suit with *eau de nil* accessories." That's my daughter, and that's Morris's father.'

Deirdre could think of nothing nice to say about the grinning nuptial celebrants so she pointed to Morris's father and said,

'He's quite tall, isn't he?'

A bitter silence filled the room. Then Morris's grandmother flicked over a few pages to the last page and lifted out a pile of unmounted photographs.

'This is Morris and his girl friend taken at Clacton. That's him with his friend Manny – God rest his soul. That's him with his sweetheart again. That's Leda by herself – such a sweet girl at times. She's probably with him now, come to think of it. They've been courting for two years now I suppose. She must be nearly seventeen by now.'

'I wonder what the time is,' said Deirdre hiding a yawn with a tanned fist.

Morris's grandmother raised her old feet in slippers and began the slow walk to the mantelpiece. Deirdre jumped up solicitously and collided with the old lady, then sank back in her chair in embarrassment.

'Five and twenty to.'

'Seven?'

'Eight, dear.'

'But Morris said he'd be here by half-past six.'

'That doesn't mean anything. He's a funny little chap – disappears for weeks at a time sometimes but he always comes back to his old Nan sooner or later. He knows there'll always be a smile and a hot dinner waiting for him here. Mind you it's only in the last five years or so—'

Deirdre thinking 'belt up belt up belt up'—

'—that he'd go out at all. He used to think everyone was looking at him in the street. He never went to school you know – I used to pay a woman to come in and teach him every day. I worked for my brother-in-law, he had an eel and pie business in Brockley, to pay her. When the doctors told us there was no hope of him growing up normal size, his mother didn't want to know. I haven't seen her in fifteen years – she was my only daughter. His father wanted to apprentice him to a circus.'

Her knees creaked as she bent to pick up a ball of beige wool.

'Do you think Morris is coming?'

'I couldn't tell you, dear. If my guess is correct he's

with Leda and when they're together they forget meal-times and hours of the day and night that we lesser mortals must observe. Oh well, that's love.'

Between two shakes of her tolerant old head she saw Deirdre blunder across the room and out of the door.

Deirdre stood by the bookstall at Charing Cross Station while her vague plans of losing herself in the anonymity of the city crashed about her head. She noticed a fat ticket collector staring at her, and studied the non-existent watch on her wrist.

'Give me some sugar, baby?' said an Eastern voice in her ear.

'No,' said Deirdre. 'Go and buy some if you want it.'

'I'll give you two pounds.'

'Go away.'

'Two pounds and this valuable lady's wrist-watch.'

'Go away,' said Deirdre and fled in a haze of tears into the booking hall. From the depths of her desolation she spoke: 'Sydenham, single.'

[7]

'I don't see many small boats willing to take us to the Continent under cover of darkness.'

Morris rested his eyes on the empty grey waves and silently agreed.

'We better go back to that Bed and Breakfast place we passed. Come on then.'

'We can't possibly go there – they'll think I kidnapped you or something.'

They were standing on a narrow path through fields of mud leading to the beach. Morris shifted the duffel bag to his other shoulder and walked forward towards the sea.

'Ouch! bloody stinging nettles.'

'Oh stop moaning!'

At length they saw a brown wooden hut further along the shore to which they directed their muddy feet. Leda managed to force open one of the cracked windows, suffering only a few minor cuts and abrasions in the process. She climbed through and her foot came to rest in a small sink filled with broken glass under the window, and she pulled Morris in by his arms after her. There was a big iron stove in the centre of the floor with a chimney leading through the roof and a high wide wooden table and two wooden benches against one wall. Leda sat shivering on the table while Morris gathered the bits of wood which lay in abundance on the floor. He found a *Daily Worker* dated April 1956 with which he lit the fire and Pif sank unlamented into flame. He hung his coat over the broken window and they dragged a bench in front of the stove and sat there eating their emergency rations of chocolate. Then they lay down on the broad table and covered themselves with their jackets. A late goods train shunted down the track and stopped and the laughter of the crew died in the night. Morris looked at Leda in the light of his cigarette and saw that her dark eyelids were closed.

Leda felt her head bouncing up and down and opened her eyes to see Morris shaking her in the grey light and closed them again quickly.

'Haven't you slept enough yet?'

'It's about three o'clock in the morning.'

'No, it isn't, it's late, wake up.' He put his arm round her and started kissing her. Leda groaned and turned away from him but he persisted so she lay with her eyes tight shut pretending to be asleep. Morris shook her hard and she began to cry quietly while the malevolent little man mocked her.

> 'Cry baby cry
> Poke your finger in your eye
> And then tell your mother
> It wasn't I.'

She thought of her mother and wanted to open her mouth and howl like a dog.

'Cry baby cry—'

She turned suddenly and bit him savagely.

'What's the matter, Leda? Don't you love me any more?'

'No, I'm tired and I want to go to sleep.'

'All right, I'll sing you to sleep.'

She thought, 'He can't even let me go to sleep by myself,' as he began to sing in his high alto.

'See how the harbour lights are shining
Far across the deep blue sea
I am going to the one who loves me.
Once I had a happy home.

Forgive me mother dear forgive me
Let me rest my head once more
Upon that soft and snowy pillow
Do not hunt me from your door.

See how my sisters stand against me
And my brothers do the same.
My father does not want to own me
My mother hangs her head in shame.

Forgive , etc.

See how my clothes are all torn
And I keep my baby warm.
Softly sleep my blue-eyed stranger,
Soon your mother will be gone.

Forgive, etc.

If you should meet my young man
Greet him with a tender smile,
For though he left me brokenhearted
He's still the father of my child.

Forgive me mother dear forgive me
Let me rest my head once more
On that soft and snowy pillow
Do not hunt me from your door.'

Some hours later Leda was awakened by a wreath of
wet cowparsley dripping on her face.

[8]

'Holy! Holy! Holy!
Lord God Almighty
Early in the morning
Our song shall rise to thee.
Holy! Holy! Holy!
Merciful and Mighty!
God in three persons
Blessed Trinity!'

Daniel modulated his heavy bass in the half empty
choirstalls and thought that somewhere in those woods
his wife was walking with the dog. They would wander
in late for meals with foolish smiles on their lips, and
buttercups dripping from the dog's collar.

Since his timely eviction of the dwarf, Elaine had
been so aloof from him that he was continually standing
in rooms mumbling half finished sentences, staring at
her departing legs.

Yesterday he had masterfully clipped on Scott's lead
only to be bitten on the wrist. It was Scott Elaine
gathered into her arms. When eventually they left the
house Scott wore no lead and Daniel walked behind
like a stranger. Stumbling over a log he found a little
colony of blue flowers.

'Orchids!' he cried.

Elaine's smile disillusioned him and she recited:

'When little elves have cut themselves
Or mouse has hurt her tail,
Or froggie's arm has come to harm
This herb will never fail.'

'What on earth are you talking about?'
'It's Selfheal, not orchids.'
'Oh.'

'Holy! Holy! Holy!
All the saints adore thee!
Casting down their golden crowns
Into the glassy sea . . .'

Daniel realized from the sudden crescendo and cessation of the organ and discreet giggles that he alone of the choir had been singing with the sopranos.

[9]

Deirdre lay abandoned in grief on the verge of the Sidcup Bypass with her face in a rainbow petrol puddle. 'I'll count to twenty then I'll do it,' she thought. One Two Three Four Five Six Seven Eight Nine Ten Eleven Twelve Thirteen Fourteen Fifteen Sixteen Seventeen Eighteen Eighteen and a quarter Eighteen and a half Eighteen and three quarters Eighteen point two five Eighteen point seven five . . . She raised herself on one arm and watched the leaping motorbikes and knew she couldn't do it.

She felt someone shake her and lift her under the shoulders and drag her languid feet into a car and slam the door. She lay back in the back seat with her eyes closed. There were two people in the front seat and they seemed to be telephoning.

The chairs at Sidcup Police Station are hard and Deirdre sat upon one in despair looking into the eyes of the kindly police officer, not hearing a word he said. She began to cry.

'I wish I was dead. I wish I was dead.'

'Don't we all,' said the police officer.

Then her father was in the doorway in his long Pakamac with a drop of rain on his nose. On the way home in the car he said, 'Your mother's been worried sick. Look, you're going to have to pull your socks up if you're going to get your A-Levels – which you are. I know it's not easy but you know you can always come to me if you're in any sort of difficulties. That's what fathers are for, aren't they?'

'I suppose so. It's the least they can do after bringing people into this lousy world.'

'I didn't ask to be born either you know,' said her father sharply.

And Deirdre finally entered on big wet legs the disillusioned adult world.

[10]

Morris ran down the wet street and dragged open the 'phone-box door and as the skies cleared in faraway Deptford his grandmother shuffled to answer the telephone's ring.

'Hello, Nan, it's me. Is Deirdre there?'

'No. She left last night.'

'Where did she go?'

'How should I know? She just ran out when I was showing her some snaps. She seemed upset about something.'

'What photographs? The ones of Leda?'

'Maybe. I don't know. I showed her quite a few so she may have seen one or two of Leda.'

'In your unobtrusive way you've ruined quite a few people's lives, haven't you?' said Morris and replaced the receiver.

He went into a shop and bought a tin of beans, two packets of soup, two bars of chocolate, a loaf and butter and a tin opener. Then he remembered there was no fresh water and bought six bottles of coke.

'Camping, sonny?' asked the shopkeeper.

Morris grinned and nodded.

Milk he stole from someone's doorstep and came home singing across the mud to find Leda had lit the fire and was sweeping the floor with a bundle of twigs.

'My mother would be surprised if she could see me now – all domesticated.'

She had forced the door too and it stood open to the sunshine. The gleaming baked beans bubbled in their tin as they stood on the hot stove. Leda dipped her hand in and ate a few – they tasted of woodsmoke. She stood in the doorway watching Morris disappear further down the beach. A gaunt gull hung in the blue sky above the sound of the sea while the pebbles rose and sank with the tide. Yellow horned poppies grew among tufts of sharp grass and the sun reflected off a piece of broken glass half buried in sand. Only the cries of the gulls and the sway of the sea – Leda remembered the baked beans and pulled them from the stove just in time.

Morris materialized from behind the trucks carrying a home-made bow and arrows.

'After breakfast I'm going hunting,' he said.

'Hunting what?'

'Gulls, cormorants, sharks, whales. They'll all fall prey to my deadly arrows.'

'You wouldn't, would you?'

Morris put down his bow and laughed and dipped his fingers into the hot tin.

'Our money won't last for ever you know,' he said through a mouthful of beans. 'If we don't find a boat we may have to stay here indefinitely and we don't want to waste all our money on necessities. And if we do find a boat, it's going to cost money. We've got to make use of the natural resources of the place. Water for instance – I'm going to dig a channel from the sea and build a filter so we can drink fresh water. You can cook gulls' eggs and we can organize raids on orchards and gardens.'

'I refuse to eat gulls' eggs. You've got hundreds of pounds and I'm supposed to live on birds' eggs.'

'Seasoned with herbs and seaweed they're delicious.'

In the afternoon they went swimming. They waded a few steps into the sea and it suddenly caught Morris with a cold smack under the arms, so he swam slowly beside Leda as she walked through the waves and then she swam forward until she was like a gull perishing on the tip of a wave. When she returned, shaking the salt from her eyes and floating calm on clear sea, Morris, smitten with jealousy, grabbed her legs and ducked her under. She came up laughing but they walked in silence up the sands.

Leda hung their wet things on a twisted thorn tree to dry. The hot wind lifted their cigarette smoke and dispersed it over the changing pebbles. Leda felt the salt dry on her back and looked at Morris lying white as a polished bone on the sand and wished he was bigger. He never tanned even in the most clement weather. His black hair stuck up in wet shiny points and his lovely expressionless eyes stared into the sun. Impotent handfuls of sand trailed from his fingers.

Leda got up and walked to the hut to get a magazine and as she lifted her hand to the door she saw a face disappear behind a clump of reeds and heard running feet scrape up the pebbles. She swallowed a scream and leaned against the door with the blood bashing in her head. His eyes told her he was not the Law. They were pale blue eyes floating in a brown face and yellowish stubble fringed his small wet mouth.

'Just a tramp, I should imagine,' said Morris when she told him and continued digging the moat of his castle. She turned and walked away from him into the sea.

A line of swans on the sinking tide sailed where the

sunset seemed less harsh, their tarry feet beating beneath the gold water and his Leda white and radiant with her head in flames floated among them.

That night Leda lay awake with that face with its pale floating eyes hovering on the edge of her brain.

What she did not know was that even then he was watching her.

[11]

Elaine paused in gathering an armful of foxgloves and broke off two blossoms and balanced them on the tips of Scott's black ears. He flicked them off and they lay torn among last year's broken beechmast.

'Fairies' hats,' thought Elaine and she thought of Morris and a long ago night under the stars and the smell of crushed foxgloves in the soft rain of West Wickham. A faraway cuckoo's call recalled her thoughts and calling Scott she turned homewards to get Daniel's tea.

She could feel cold disapproval on the back of her neck as she stood with the tin opener in her hand.

'I didn't know there was a shortage of peas this summer.'

'These don't take so long,' said Elaine nervously putting them on the stove.

'Elaine! This is no kind of meal to offer a man after a hard day's work. When a man comes home at night he expects a decent meal,' said Daniel, the tin opener twitching convulsively in his hand. 'Not this tinned rubbish.'

Without turning round she heard his individual fruit pie crumple in his hand and the click of the refuse bin.

'I'll fry myself an egg,' he said and pushed her out of the way with the frying pan, but, alas, the cupboard held only a tub of glacé cherries and half a jar of peanut butter.

Daniel felt hunger filling his stomach, flowing along his arms and legs and pounding in his brain. He grabbed Elaine and pushed her to the floor, and holding her with his knees, opened her head like a tin of peas.

Elaine lay for half an hour with blood running into her eyes. She got up and went to the telephone and through a red haze dialled the doctor's number.

'Express Dairy Company. Can I help you?'

'I want the doctor.'

'I'm sorry, this is the Express Dairy Company.'

'Can you tell me where I can get the doctor?'

'I can only suggest you dial 999. This is the Express Dairy Company.'

Click.

This time Elaine, fighting against the jagged red pain in her head, made sure she got the correct combination of figures. She wiped the blood from her eye as the faraway telephone rang on its dusted cradle.

'Express Dairy Company. Can I help you?'

Elaine crawled upstairs to her bed and lay across it. She was sure death was very near at hand and wished only that Scott was there to share it but no quick spurt of claws on the unpolished floor answered her faint cries. Luckily a kindly neighbour, happening past with the Parish Magazine – 'It's fourpence but most people prefer to pay sixpence' – noticed the disorder of the kitchen and entering on trembling feet summoned an ambulance and bathed the wounded brow with a wet doyley.

She couldn't help but feel a surge of pride as she walked beside the trolley into the antisepsis of the Out-patients and frowned at many an impeding plaster cast and crutch. She was allowed to sit on a special steel and canvas chair outside the room where Elaine was taken.

'I'll be standing by here if necessary, Sister,' she said to a ward orderly.

Daniel strode in silence the short cut through the field to the village, and stood in the bar of the King's Head and in the silence that had fallen ordered a Double Diamond. He drank it with blood on his concealed hand, a crushed marsh marigold clinging to his shoe and the added distinction of being the only person in the bar who didn't know he had murdered his wife. There was a general sigh and cough of satisfaction as P.C. Bedford tapped him on the shoulder and led him out for questioning.

'I wonder if you could excuse me just for a moment?' said Daniel and at a nod from his superior officer the constable opened a green door on the left and closed it behind Daniel.

Daniel took his hands from his trouser pockets and washed them in the little basin with a bar of pink soap. He noticed that he was the first to use it. With what infinite regret he watched the red and pink stream slowly down the white. 'And now,' he said re-entering the room, 'perhaps you will be so good as to tell me what this is all about.'

'Your wife, sir.'

'Elaine? Why? What's she done?'

'There has been an accident. Your wife is in hospital with serious head injuries. What do you know about this?'

The sergeant saw Daniel pale and he swayed on his feet. The constable pushed a chair forward but Daniel rejected it with his foot.

'Where's Elaine? Where's my wife? I demand to know!'

He grabbed the sergeant's lapels and shook them. The constable pushed the chair into the backs of his legs and he sat down suddenly.

'That's better,' said the sergeant.

'Now, sir, when did you last see your wife?'

'This morning about 8.30 before I left for work.'

'You haven't been home tonight?'

'Well, in a manner of speaking I have. I was practically outside my own gate when I saw a friend of my wife's in the garden, so I went on to the pub.'

'Who was this friend?'

'Chap named Todd – a dwarf.'

Action sprang into the sergeant's eyes. 'Thank you, sir. You've been most helpful. Your wife is in St Mary's Hospital. You can go now. Constable Bedford will drive you if you like.'

Daniel shook his head and blundered towards the door, trying to control his shaking face.

'Just one more thing, sir,' called the sergeant. 'Do you recognize this?'

'Looks rather like a tin opener to me,' said Daniel, forcing himself to look at the weapon which by now held only the kindly neighbour's prints, for wishing to preserve the evidence she had wrapped it carefully in a duster.

Daniel now did one of the few actions of which he was to feel really proud for the rest of his life. He walked back to the King's Head and finished his drink.

[12]

Gloria Margolis sighed as she handed over thirty
guineas for a red leather suit, for which she would weep
at Yom Kippur.

At times, especially during Assembly, D. K. McGovern was tempted to confess the intolerable burden of guilt that weighed upon her soul. She was unable to partake of Holy Communion, not being in a state of grace. She was taking a Domestic Science Course in addition to her A-Level subjects.

> 'Once to every man and nation
> Comes the moment to decide
> In the strife of truth with falsehood
> For the good or evil side.
> Some great cause God's New Messiah
> Offering each the bloom or blight
> And that choice goes on forever
> Twixt that darkness and that light.
>
> Then it is the brave man chooses
> While the coward stands aside
> Though his portion be the scaffold—'

She closed her eyes and saw a throne, and on one side those who had accepted the bloom streamed in in shining garments, albeit some had just been cut down from the scaffold, and those who had chosen the blight shuffled into the shadows.

'By the light of burning martyrs
Christ Thy bleeding feet we track
Toiling up new Calvaries ever
With the Cross that turns not back.'

She opened her eyes and saw Miss Lambe parching like a lily on the platform in the intense light of August.

After prayers she changed, and, the muscles of a well co-ordinated body rippling under her regulation black swimsuit, she plunged into the newly finished swimming bath, catching her foot on a raw edge of concrete as she jumped. She crouched on the bottom of the bath with the blue water roaring past her ears and waves beating in her head while great bubbles burst from her throat. Her past did not float before her, only a voice calling dimly, 'Deirdre, Deirdre,' floated across the waters.

'I come O Lord,' and strong angel arms lifted her and she was borne gently through pastures of light into ultimate peace.

She felt her head spinning like a white globe into eternity and opened her bursting eyes to see an angel in a wet track suit kneeling beside her, dripping on to her face. Deirdre turned her head away and was sick.

In grim silence Miss Baker pulled her to her feet and led her to the changing room and handed her a towel.

'Now perhaps you will be so kind as to explain what you were doing in the swimming bath during a First Form swimming period?'

Deirdre became aware of wet little faces flickering round the edge of the door and disappearing.

'Didn't you see my note?' she asked, not daring to raise her eyes.

'This?' Miss Baker held between her finger and thumb a piece of lined paper. 'I assumed it was part of your literature homework.'

Deirdre got up and taking with her the letter, saying, 'I cannot live a lie any longer,' departed behind the shower curtain.

At break D. K. McGovern stood outside Miss Lambe's office. Her hand faltered twice towards the door before knocking. Then she stood in the room which commanded a fine view of the hockey field and had a headless china shepherdess standing on the mantelpiece. She stood in front of the leather-topped desk behind which sat Miss Lambe swathed in a dress of muted purple and yellow flowered silk, her grey utility haircut not enhanced by rimless glasses.

'Do sit down, Deirdre. To what do I owe the pleasure of this visit?' she asked smiling and stroking a teak ruler.

Deirdre sitting awkwardly on the edge of a chair cleared her throat and twisted her tie.

'Well?' Miss Lambe said with yellowing teeth through her faded smile.

'There's something I must tell you. I decided in prayers this morning,' and Deirdre, hoping her reference to the morning's hymn would soften her headmistress's heart, told humbly and haltingly of her complicity in the spending of the stolen money. When she stumbled over her words or hesitated Miss Lambe made no attempt to help her, neither did she give any indication that she was listening. She merely stroked her ruler.

'I met this man in the park – well he was a sort of dwarf really – if you know what I mean. What I mean is – I don't usually talk to men in the park unless it's my father or my uncle or something but I didn't know he was a man—'

At the end of this anecdote Deirdre was bathed in tears while Miss Lambe's plump fingers with their triangular nails stroked the ruler in silence. At length she spoke. 'I don't really know what to say to you, Deirdre. This is really a police matter – but as they say they have a pretty shrewd idea of the identity of the thief anyway I don't see that anything would be gained by involving one of our girls – the school's reputation would of necessity suffer. I shall have to call a staff meeting. Meanwhile I suggest you consider the swimming pool as out of bounds.'

Deirdre stumbled to the door and twisted the handle in her wet hand for what seemed like ten minutes before it would open and she stood on the edge of a corridor filled with screaming girls and milk bottles, and the smell of milk and wet straws was the scent of despair in her nose.

She walked round the library stopping now and then in front of a shelf where the blue, red and green books blurred together in front of her swimming eyes. The confessional with Miss Lambe had been inconclusive and unsatisfactory. She didn't know what to do with herself. GCE drew near and she had done no revision. Every night she packed her briefcase with papers and books and sat in her bedroom with books piled in front of her staring blankly until late at night.

'Deirdre's working too hard,' said her mother to her father as she came down from taking her a cup of cocoa. Her father nodded in approval because he thought people should work too hard.

Deirdre opened her Gallic Wars and thought about Morris. He was the only man who had ever paid her a compliment. Then she remembered a Maths master who had praised her neat graphs in the third year. She ran her fingers through her short hair as if to scratch out the memory of what had occurred at Morris's grandmother's and the subsequent humiliations since she had met him. She made little holes in the book with her compasses, thinking about him.

'He's physically repulsive. Freaks like him shouldn't be allowed to go about ruining other people's lives,' she told herself trying to forget the sweat that sprang to her hands and the smile that lingered when she got on the bus after he kissed her hovering cheek.

The August moon hung heavy over the wet garden and Deirdre noticed with regret her mud-caked hockey boots slumped crookedly in a corner. There was a time . . .

She heard her father downstairs switch off the Epilogue and she packed her books into her briefcase and clicked it shut and went into the bathroom. Her parents' toothbrushes stood erect and martial red and blue on either side of the plastic glassholders, and her own slouched pale green in the glass. She stared at them for some time before applying the pallid blue toothpaste and a sudden thought struck her of mothers all over the country buying toothpaste to strengthen the enamel of children's teeth who would rather be dead.

As she bent over the chair to kiss her mother good night she knocked an ashtray from its arm, and her father saying good night reached out to ruffle her hair but his hand just missed.

When she lay in bed the tears, which she seemed to be

continually blinking from her eyes, overflowed and she let them run softly down her face.

Her mother stood shaking daylight through the open curtains with the sun on her face calling for the third time.

'Deirdre! You're going to be late,' and Deirdre who lay with her eyes closed having heard the first time, thought, 'I cannot go to school today.' So that when she stood in her buttoned-up mac in the kitchen gulping tea she did not give her mother time to comment on a mac in a heat wave but waved as she jumped on her bicycle. When she got to the station she abandoned her bicycle and mac and blossomed forth in the booking hall in a straight white dress.

From Charing Cross Station she walked past the shining fountains of Trafalgar Square, ignoring the drops that fell on her and about her feet and the pigeons on the dusty stone, to Leicester Square, where, turning down a side street, she was soon lost.

After a while she became very thirsty, and being broke, was sorely tempted by a bruised orange in the gutter of Berwick Market but could not bring herself to pick it up.

Her eye was attracted by a display of books and magazines outside a little shop and she crossed the road to look at them. Disgusted yet fascinated she lingered. She was examining the cover of a book called *Painful Pleasures* when she felt someone watching her and looking up saw a bearded young man of about twenty-four standing in the doorway.

'Antithesis,' she said with a nervous giggle pointing to the title of the book.

'No. Flagellation,' he replied in a north country accent. Then, 'Do you want anything in particular?'

'I'm just looking, for the moment, thank you,' she said in her mother's voice.

'Why don't you come inside and look round then?'

'All right.'

Inside the shop was very small with shelves of books and racks of magazines round the walls. There was a table and chair at the back.

'Sit down,' he said smiling and pulling the chair out for her. Then his attention was taken by several customers who drifted about the shop selecting and exchanging magazines. Deirdre was rather shocked to see that they looked like ordinary men. When the shop was empty he said, 'Where do you work?'

'I don't.'

'Sensible girl. Wish I didn't have to. Would you like to earn some money?'

'I don't know.'

'Well, my colleague will be in in a minute and we can discuss it with him. I'm John,' and he held out his hand for Deirdre to shake and introduce herself.

A few minutes later a dark-haired man with a pock-marked face, sunglasses and suède jacket walked in.

'Marcel, this young lady would like to earn some money,' said John.

Marcel looked long at Deirdre then back at John.

'What exactly would I have to do?' asked Deirdre.

'Are you interested in photography? No? Well, we're photographers, and I think you would have a very photogenic face. Yes – especially from the back. I'd like to take a few shots of you and if they turn out well I

46

would consider using you as a regular model. Interested?'

Deirdre picked up one of the magazines.

'You mean pictures like this, don't you?'

'Smart girl. Yes.'

Deirdre said nothing so he went on. 'There are two types – straight photographs such as these in underwear, lingerie, etc., and erotic such as these, a man and a girl – two girls, etc. For the straight we talk in pounds but for the other we start talking in fivers. What do you think?'

'No.'

'You could earn yourself quite a bit. Why not think about it and drop in and tell us tomorrow. Would you do that?'

'I don't know if I could – I'd probably have to come in school uniform if I came at all—'

'School uniform! That's marvellous. Do you think you could?'

'Perhaps. But what's so marvellous about school uniform?'

'It's very popular for export. Some time tomorrow then? Good girl. There's just one thing – will you promise to keep this a secret? Don't tell anyone, not even your best friend. Promise?'

'Yes,' said Deirdre. 'See you tomorrow then. Goodbye.'

Marcel followed her to the door.

'If you disappoint me I shall be very – disappointed,' he said with a smile that scarcely stretched his mouth.

Deirdre knew that if she caught a train fairly soon she would be able to get home and change while her mother was out and get to school in time for afternoon register. Her spirits had lightened considerably.

On the way home, GCE in mind, she mentally revised. Science, the tape-worm.

'It bathes in digested foodstuffs,' she said as the train rattled past London Bridge.

[14]

Elaine. Elaine. The foxgloves wither in their jar. It is the third week of solitude for Daniel in the dusty house and the hot days heave towards the end of summer. A few more days and Elaine will be driven, her thin legs heavy with tartan rugs, to the home near Maidstone where she will conceivably spend the next sixty years.

Daniel had not been charged with attempted murder or even with causing grevious bodily harm. While detectives sat by Elaine's bedside, notebooks poised, she had muttered through cracked lips, 'Morris, Morris,' and when questioned as to her attacker had still murmured only 'Morry'. To the police, who unknown to the Press had a pretty shrewd idea, to put it in their own words, of the identity of the mysterious and savage toddler, this was enough to confirm Daniel's story and intensify their search for Morris.

Daniel swirled the rotten stem of a foxglove in the brown water and remembered her lying white beneath the red blanket and saying, 'You know although I'm considered a simpleton I don't feel so very different in myself.' A seed catalogue fluttered to the floor. His colleagues at Lincoln's Inn had been very sympathetic in his tribulation, and as he said to Elaine, 'People at the office have been saying I look thin and ill,' which was untrue.

Daniel got up and went to bed four times and then on the fifth day he had a bath and shaved and dressed in a dark blue suit which Elaine hated. He had nice legs but concealed in his solicitor's suit they might just as well have been macaroni or goat's hooves.

He drove to the hospital with a case containing some of Elaine's clothes. It was Sunday and as he walked across the sunny entrance court he met a procession of patients wrapped in red blankets and some in wheel-chairs being conducted to the hospital chapel. It was apparently the Harvest Festival and in their hands they bore gifts of fruit and flowers, cornflowers and Michael-mas daisies. A lady with her head swathed in white bandages carried a giant marrow. As they descended the stairs she tripped and it fell from her plastered fingers and split, spilling its seeds on the hot stone.

The ward was empty except for Elaine and an old lady who was shortly to be moved to the geriatric ward. Daniel walked past the empty beds and put the case on the end of Elaine's bed. 'Hello, darling,' he said and pecked at the top of her hair. He could not kiss her because he did not know if she knew that he was responsible for her injuries. On an earlier visit soon after she had regained consciousness after the effect of the drugs had worn off, he had taken her hand and said, 'Elaine, often after an accident of this sort, the ex-perience leaves a mark on the mind. At first you may find yourself thinking all sorts of terrible things and even accusing innocent people of harming you or trying to harm you. You must put all these thoughts right out of your mind and concentrate on getting well and strong again.'

A nurse drew the curtains round Elaine's bed and withdrew behind them to help her dress. Daniel went and stood by the window, his feet felt hot in their socks, and looking over the tops of a vase of chrysanthemums he saw the fields yellow with corn and charlock and heard voices singing:

> 'We plough the fields and scatter
> The good seed on the land
> But it is fed and watered
> By God's Almighty hand.'

He heard the sound of quiet sobbing and pulling back the green curtain saw Elaine sitting on the edge of the bed with her stockings flopping round her ankles, crying while she surveyed her helpless legs.

'You forgot a suspender belt,' said the nurse. 'Just like a man!'

'Yes, he is rather like a man, isn't he?' said Elaine.

'We'll have to collect it on the way to Maidstone.' Daniel swore to himself. He had not wanted Elaine to see the house again, or Scott for whom she had asked constantly. She had his picture in her locket. Daniel had promised to bring him to visit her whenever he possibly could, although he had already ascertained that dogs were not allowed at Fairhaven Nursing Home.

Elaine was ready now and she stood in a dark green dress at the end of the bed. Daniel gave the nurse a five-pound box of chocolates and thanked her and her colleagues for all they had done for his wife. Then took Elaine's arm and they walked downstairs and across the gravel to the car. He looked at her as she sat beside him in the car and seeing again the faint smudge of freckles under her eyes wondered if perhaps Maidstone was not a mistake and if they could be happy together again. He felt no guilt because (a) he knew that solicitors do not try to murder their wives, (b) he had been provoked for months, and (c) he had convinced himself that Morris had done it anyway or was at least responsible for it. Then he remembered that she might betray him and also that less attention is paid to the allegations of mental patients. He decided to visit her fairly often and take her expensive presents and that way she would probably be happier. He stopped the car outside their gate and locked the door and hurried into the house. He returned in five minutes with a black suspender belt dangling from his pocket.

All the way down the road she could hear Scott, shut in the kitchen, barking and wailing. She put on her stockings with great difficulty. Neither spoke and Daniel turned on the radio. It was Family Favourites, a programme which he normally disliked. They drove through the quiet streets of Maidstone and stopped outside a pair of iron gates in a high wall. 'Fairhaven Nursing Home' was painted in white Gothic letters on a wooden sign. The gate was opened by a man in a grey uniform and they drove past borders blazing with calceolaria to the grey house at the end of the drive. Two or three wheelchairs stood on the lawn.

The matron met them on the steps and shook hands with Elaine. Daniel caught sight of his and Elaine's reflections in a mirror above a silver bowl of tea roses on a polished table. She looked so vulnerable with her soft straight brown hair and white face that he was on the point of dropping the case, picking up Elaine and running back to the car. Instead he followed, with his hand on the hollow of Elaine's back, the matron along a corridor, up a flight of stairs and into a small room. The walls were distempered pale green and there was also a table and a bed with a silk eiderdown. A red strand of Virginia creeper blew across the window and on the wall was a small reproduction of Lorenzetti's *St Francis of Assisi Reproaching Brother Pig*. At this point Elaine's face disintegrated into tears and the matron motioned Daniel out of the room. A nurse came to help her to unpack. As the door closed behind them Daniel heard Elaine say, 'I shall be sending for my dog soon.'

'Oh well, I'm not sure if – I don't know anything about it.'

'Yes, it's perfectly all right. He'll be coming in a few days. He can sleep here with me.'

Daniel and the matron exchanged looks of despair and reassurance. The matron laid a puce hand on Daniel's blue arm. 'She'll get over it when she's settled down a bit. We often have trouble at first. There was one lady, you may have seen her in the garden, in the invalid chair, wearing a black band on her arm, who talked of nothing but her husband for the first three weeks, then he married someone else, eventually, and now she never mentions him. It would probably be best to have the dog put to sleep – it would save a lot of trouble. Of course, we have some budgerigars here so I'll encourage your wife to take an interest in them.'

They had reached the gate now and matron stood serenely in her glacé kid C-fitting extra width shoes smiling into the setting sun as the car drove out of sight.

[15]

Four days later Daniel drove to Maidstone again. Beyond the nurse's thermometer pointing through the bougainvillaea stood Elaine in a green Thai silk dress, leaning with one hand on a stone bench. A small pond stagnated at her narrow feet. Daniel walked down to join her and kissed her on the cheek.

'You're looking well,' he said. The patch of hair which had been removed in hospital had almost grown again.

'So are you.'

'I'm glad you think so. People at the office have been saying I'm looking thin and ill.'

'Oh.' There followed a pause in which there was nothing to do but look into the water. Daniel discerned glittering faintly below the surface a sheet of wire netting.

'Why the wire netting? I mean it's not as though any children are likely to fall in, is it?'

'A lady put her head in the spin-drier last month!'

'Oh – I see.'

A goldfish swam through the wire and into a trail of dark weed. Daniel looked away – he had gone off goldfish ever since an afternoon as a boy when he stood transfixed in front of a pet-shop window for half an hour watching a goldfish eat a watersnail, its mouth expanded pulling the snail from its shell. Daniel and Elaine looked at each other and what latent love and feelings of tenderness he had felt in the car and guilt through the heavy scent of the bougainvillaea had gone and he looked at her and thought – I do not find you attractive, you bore me. You are mentally sick and I find you and this place distasteful. Then he thought of her putting on the green silk dress in anticipation of his coming and also the delicate shoes. When she bent to pick up a stone he saw her white neck and thought, 'Well, the backs of all necks are vulnerable,' but his was not.

'I've been thinking, Daniel. Shall we go to Spain next year?'

'I thought Spain was out of the question for you because (a) the bullfights and (b) it's a Fascist government?'

'Yes, but I know you've always wanted to go, that's why I suggested it.'

Daniel knew he should say, 'Yes, dear. Yes, we will go and have a wonderful time and you will get well in the sun and it will be like old times when we were first married.' But instead he said:

'Can't you see, Elaine, it's no use. We have nothing any more. And anyway I don't know if you'd be well enough.'

'I'm a voluntary patient.'

'If we had had children things might have been different but there's nothing to hold us together. I'm not asking for my freedom, Elaine, but you must realize that I have been professionally harmed.'

A fly gleamed blue on a water-lily leaf and Elaine's eyes darkened and her lips shook. Had Daniel been a nurse he would have recognized this as a sign of impending hysteria but he was not and so noticed nothing except little lines had formed beneath her eyes. Fortunately a nurse pushing a trolley across the grass towards them put a tablet from her white pocket between Elaine's fluttering lips and moving briskly among the frail china poured two cups of tea. The roses on the cups, the delicacy of the scones—

'We generally always have plain china,' said Elaine. 'This is in honour of you.'

'Do you generally have plain china or do you always have plain china?' said Daniel after a mouthful of scone, smiling at the nurse as if to say this is delicious and it is many a long day since – so that she was moved to remark to another nurse in passing, 'What a charming man.'

'Generally always.'

The bread and butter faded from the plate. 'The clicking of our teeth mercifully prevents other things such as talk,' thought Elaine. Later when the trolley had gone back over the newly cut lawn leaving trails of grass cuttings she said to her husband:

'You haven't mentioned my dog.'

'Oh Scott – he's all right. Mrs Snell feeds him.'

'Does he miss me very much?'

'No, I don't think so. He seems to have settled down all right. He wouldn't eat for a couple of days,' said Daniel remembering the times he had knelt and was still kneeling in front of the dog basket pleading and shouting, offering steak and chicken and frozen mince to the silent dog and all the time his hand hovering towards the telephone to call the vet and put an end to it all and he had hugged Scott when he had consented to take a boiled sweet from his hand and Scott had bared his teeth in contempt. He had taken to staying out late to avoid Scott's eyes.

'Yes, he seems perfectly happy,' he repeated.

'Good,' said Elaine, wishing to hear that Scott lay in his basket pining with his head on his paws and a tear glistening on his black snout.

'Well, I must love you and leave you,' said Daniel.

'What an unfortunate thing to say.'

'I'll see you next month. I can find my own way to the gate. Good-bye, Elaine,' and he kissed her on the lips briefly.

Letters from relations and other ill-wishers and friends lay in the writing case at Elaine's feet and among them lay photographs of Scott standing in his prime and majesty of fur, a dog Adonis in the falling leaves. Even my dog does not miss me – two days' token fast, two minutes' silence for the fallen dead who bleed in their graves through two million eternities and when there is no more blood, rot. She was going to tear up the photographs but did not. She walked to the pond – the wire netting beneath her feet was firm. Elaine hesitated at the door of the lounge where on chintz chairs the wealthy infirm of mind sat, the late sunshine reflecting off the glass of a tapestry firescreen or illuminating an old head bent over a jigsaw. She went upstairs to where her friend Marjorie sat enthroned on uncut moquette, knitting a layette, it was not known for whom. She wore an olive cashmere cardigan – very decolleté, and a large tweed skirt and strong shoes were laced upon her feet. Elaine could not remember her friend's name so she smiled as she entered the room because she knew there was an affinity there, and Marjorie, who sometimes called her Catherine, smiled back.

'Someone came to see me today.'

'A relative?'

'No. Just somebody I used to know – I was married to him once.'

'Did he think you were looking well?'

'Yes, but now I have rather a headache. I think I shall ask nurse for a codeine.'

'Be careful, Catherine. The body provides its own sedatives and stimulants; it is easy to become addicted. Even the harmless aspirin—'

Elaine sat beside her friend and remembered that she had wanted to boast to Daniel.

'I have made this friend. Her name is— We share a lot of interests,' but his coldness had prevented her. Evening fell on the Kentish garden, and beyond the garden in the long green grass by the stream ducks were beginning to quack as the pail was carried through the sorrel and sorrow of scattered feathers, and the brown bran steamed bringing joy to their beaks.

'—and after the bran, what then?' thought Elaine.

She fell silent and still through the notes of the echoing handbell and when the nurse came to look for her she had forgotten where she was and suffered herself to be led away and her hands placed under the running tap and her face splashed with warm water from a sponge and verbena soap, and then to her room.

And after the codeine, what then?

Two hours later she woke from a dream of dark and writhing torment and went downstairs to join the other patients in the lounge.

As the car waited for the amber light at Sevenoaks Daniel remembered with surprise and unbelief those times when he had said with tears in his adequate eyes, 'I don't know why you love me, Elaine. I'm not half good enough for you. I'm unworthy of you.' Surely he must have known he was twenty times better than she. And the ruined parties of their early marriage when he had hissed at her, 'Go on – dance with him if you want to. I don't care,' and sat in a corner glaring into his glass aware of being a laughing-stock but unable to do anything about it. And he remembered the way, when she crouched, her legs flaring from the shin-bone made elongated hearts. But any tenderness left was cancelled by the thought that at the age of thirty-four and with domestic help in the house, she had little cause to crouch. Elaine's crouching days were over.

On the way down Station Road he overtook the vicar and reversing, offered him a lift, which the Rev Lunch, gathering up his skirts, accepted.

'I've just been to see my wife,' said Daniel.

'Oh, how is she? I must pop along myself one of these days.'

'Well, frankly, Vicar, Elaine's deteriorating. She seems to be losing her grip entirely.'

Ted Lunch shook his head sadly. A crumb of the Sacrament adhered to his stock but he did not know. When he got out at the wisteria-hung vicarage he shook Daniel's hand and said:

'See you at choir practice, old man. We'll really have to get to grips with that "Prepare thyself Zion".'

Daniel drove through the village humming:

> 'The purest da da da da da da
> The fairest da da da da da da
> Prepare thyself Zion
> With tender affection
> The purest, the fairest
> This day to receive.'

The house was clean and cool sullied only by the *Sunday Times* upon the floor. Under a white cloth a salad reposed awaiting him, the tomatoes cut into flowers and a drop of water at the base of each light green leaf. Scott was apparently out. He checked his watch – he would have time to eat, bath, shave and change in ample time before going to the Rotarians' dinner. With a piece of cold ham in his mouth he placed a record of Kathleen Ferrier singing excerpts from the St Matthew Passion on the turntable and remembered Elaine once saying: 'How can you sit there with some poor dead calf's tongue in your mouth listening to religious music? You wouldn't like it if someone ate Kathleen Ferrier's tongue or St Matthew's.'

'Don't be silly, dear,' Daniel had said.

'Grief for sin rends the guilty heart within,'

sang Kathleen Ferrier from both speakers of the stereo equipment.

Much later that evening the telephone rang and Daniel, jovial from his dinner, answered with a cheery shout which he moderated when he heard it was the matron of Fairhaven Nursing Home.

'There is a dog here, Mr. Pyke, which your wife claims is hers.'

'Dog? What sort of dog?'

'It's a black Chow.'

Daniel looked at the empty basket with defeat in his face.

'Will it be all right if I pick him up in the morning?'

It would be all right, and as he put down the receiver

Daniel was aware of a distinct feeling of disappointment which he could only put down to the fact that, although it shocked him, he had hoped the matron was going to say that Elaine was dead.

[16]

Whether of men or angels the voices were when he woke Daniel could not divine, then he realized he had left the radio on and it was the Glasgow Orpheus Choir. He lay in bed elevated above dogs and sick wives listening to 'All in the April Evening' deeply moved by the heartbreaking way they sang:

> 'All in the April evening
> April airs were abroad.
> I saw the sheep with their lembs
> And I thought on the Lemb of God.'

Then he remembered Scott and turned over and pulled the covers over his head and tried to think of April lambs but all that came into his mind was a dead sheep caught on a bed of stones in the narrow river and minnows swimming through its swollen wool.

He got up and timed himself to dress in the nine-thirty news summary but was so dissatisfied with the result that he had a bath and slow shave and changed into a sports jacket, checked shirt, cavalry twills and a cravat with a gold horsehead pin. He cooked an elaborate breakfast of eggs, bacon, kidney and tomatoes and ate it. Then he rinsed the dishes and put them in the rack and while doing so noticed the water level in Scott's bowl had fallen and just covered the base and a black insect floated on its back on the surface.

As he drove the skies darkened and by the time he reached Maidstone he had to switch on the windscreen wipers. He ran from the car to the front door and rang the bell. The porter surveyed him with dismay as he dripped in the hall and said, 'Lovely weather for ducks,' as he led him to the Matron's room and knocked on the door. A green light flashed – the signal for entry – and Daniel did. The pink and grey pagoda of her sincere and flourishing face and hair inclined towards him as Daniel sat in a chintz chair.

'I am so sorry to bring you out all this way, Mr—' and blushed like a competent petunia when she could not remember his name. Daniel supplied it, 'Pyke', and after a few pleasantries and coffee served with Marie biscuits Daniel said, 'Where is the dog now, Miss Jeffrys?'

'Call me Matron – everyone does. He's in the West Wing with Mrs Pyke. Shall we walk through the garden? The rain has stopped.'

A few diligent patients toiled in the blazing beds of calceolarium, salvia and fuchsia.

'We are particularly proud of our garden,' said Matron, 'especially as so much of the work is done by the patients themselves.' She turned smiling upon an old lady who was weeding a border as they passed.

'You've got green fingers, Mrs Smithe,' she said, whereupon the old lady jumped up with a horrified glance at her hands, tripped over a bed of love-lies-bleeding and ran into the house where she could be heard lamenting for soap.

'So many of them have these absurd obsessions,' Matron said apologetically to Daniel, unaware that her

Cuban heels were making deep circular dents in the turf and a young man was weeping.

The West Wing with its long white-framed Georgian windows stood on a raised terrace at the top of a flight of broad stone steps. Little pools of golden water lay in the stone mouths of cupids holding the fern-filled urns and they steamed slightly as the sun dried them. Daniel followed the Matron through the open door. The hall seemed dark after the sunlight outside and their feet made little noise on the polished parquet floor, and the scent of roses filled the hall and the stairs with a faint drift of antiseptic mingling and fading.

Half-way up the stairs they were met by a distraught hatchet-faced woman, hirsute, on flying feet who clattered to a standstill when she saw them.

'Why, Nurse, whatever's the matter?' asked Matron laying a restraining hand on the overalled arm.

'The patient, Mrs Pyke, and the dog have disappeared, Matron. I've searched everywhere and I can't find them. Oh dear, what shall I do?'

'Disappeared! Good heavens, Nurse! Are you sure?'

'Disappeared?' echoed Daniel at the same time.

The nurse nodded her distracted head. 'I saw her at breakfast and she seemed very het up so I was going to give her a sedative. When I knocked on her door there was no answer and when I went in there was no one there. That's what comes of breaking rules,' she sobbed.

'Calm yourself, woman,' said Daniel, wondering bleakly if he would ever rest from troubles inflicted by Scott and Elaine.

The Matron ran downstairs followed by Daniel and the nurse and into her room where she emerged with three handbells.

'Here,' she said giving them to the nurse. 'Take one yourself and give one each to Nurse Wilkins and Nurse Fleming. Ring them throughout the building and assemble all patients and nurses in the assembly hall. Quickly now!'

'Why on earth don't you have a proper alarm system?' asked Daniel.

'It makes it so like Broadmoor.'

'Is there anything I can do?'

'Well, I think it would be best to wait until everyone is assembled. Someone may have seen your wife or she may have told someone where she was going. Mr Pyke' – laying a hand on his arm – 'I can't tell you how sorry I am all this has happened. It's not due in any way to negligence I can assure you. Our nurses are very conscientious.'

'I don't doubt it.'

Matron went to the study door and looked down the corridor. 'Ah, Marjorie!' she called to a lady passing with the throng. 'Could you spare a moment please?'

Marjorie, wearing a *décollete* brown ecru lace dress and carrying her knitting came into the room.

'Marjorie, this is Mrs Pyke's husband.'

'Ah, Mr Pyke! I've been wanting to meet you. Catherine and I are such friends.'

'Catherine?'

'Yes, she speaks of you often.'

Matron looked at Daniel and he realized that Marjorie was not quite sane.

'How typical of Elaine to choose a woman like that for her friend,' thought Daniel.

'Marjorie,' said Matron, 'I wonder if Catherine mentioned to you that she was going anywhere? You haven't seen her today, have you?'

'Certainly. We shared the morning paper at breakfast.'

'And after breakfast?'

'I retired to my room to meditate and knit and Catherine went into the garden with her dog. A magnificent beast,' she said turning to Daniel with a smile which was not returned.

'Thank you, Marjorie. Now I think you should join the others in the assembly hall.'

'Good morning, Mr Pyke,' said Marjorie smiling pleasantly as she went out, trailing a ball of pink wool behind her.

'Well, I think I had better go and address the patients. Would you care to come, Mr Pyke, or would you prefer to wait here?'

'I'll come if you don't mind.'

Daniel opened the door for her and then followed her into the assembly hall and on to a slightly raised platform. He wished he hadn't when he saw the faces turned up to listen.

The previous night while she and Marjorie had sat in the lounge playing dominoes there was a sudden barking outside the french windows, and Elaine jumped up, knocking over the little card table and scattering the dominoes on the floor, and rushed to the locked windows, pulled back the curtains and rushed to the front door. Marjorie took the opportunity of altering the scores she had been keeping on an envelope and followed her. The porter and Nurse Wilkins were trying to hold a black Chow who was jumping on his forelegs and barking and when Elaine ran out into the terrace, leaped into her outstretched arms. Elaine sat down on the steps holding him and smothering his black velvet snout and triangular ears with kisses while he jumped about and licked her face, running away backwards a few steps and then back to her and all the time barking loudly. So that Matron put her head out of her window, thinking it was a patient who suffered from delusions, and called:

'Nurse, will you please get Mr Coles inside and give him a sedative. He'll disturb the whole neighbourhood,' and was greatly shocked to see that it was a real dog.

'Good heavens! How did that dog get in? Put him outside the gate immediately, Saunders.'

'I can't catch him, Matron. He seems to have taken a fancy to Mrs Pyke here.'

'What nonsense! Two great strong men – oh sorry, Nurse Wilkins, it's you – and you can't deal with a dog.'

She banged the window resignedly and came down on to the terrace, and now some twenty patients were crowding round Scott and Elaine who sat on the steps with the late summer evening casting cool shadows on their faces.

'Do you know this dog?' she asked Elaine who raised her face radiant with happy tears and nodded.

'He's my dog – my Scott. I don't know how he got here – he must have walked.'

'Unless he came by dog-cart,' suggested a Major Mallet and laughed hilariously until his mirth gurgled to a standstill and was quenched by a look from Nurse Wilkins.

'Well, for goodness' sake everybody come inside. These late dews are treacherous.'

They all went, singly and in pairs in through the

front door and back to the lounge. Elaine sat on the chintz sofa with Scott's front paws in her hands, looking into his eyes, oblivious of Matron's voice behind her saying, 'It'll have to go, of course.'

'I knew he would come,' she said to Marjorie, tears dropping again on to her red silk kimono dressing-gown and Scott's closed eyes. She let go his paws and they thumped to the floor and his head fell on to them and he slept exhaustedly.

'Poor boy,' said Elaine. 'It's a wonder he hasn't worn his pads out.' She lifted a paw and examined the under surface; the black pad was scratched and cracked but it was not bleeding.

'Perhaps you could come into my room, Mrs Pyke, so that we could discuss what's to be done with him.'

Elaine got up and Scott immediately woke and followed them into Matron's room. A pile of brochures, certification papers, death certificates and other correspondence on her desk showed that she was ever busy with the administrative affairs of Fairhaven. She switched on the desk lamp and sat behind it, and indicating the chair opposite said, 'Do sit down, Mrs Pyke.' Elaine sat down with Scott's head in her lap, and her hand on his head and tried to listen to what Matron was saying.

'You realize of course, Mrs Pyke, that doggie – er, Scottie, can't stay here. It wouldn't be fair on the other patients. What I think would be the best plan is, I'll ring up your husband and ask him to come and take the dog home as soon as possible. Don't you think that would be the best plan? You really should try to forget about him – it's not healthy to be so devoted to an animal. Nurse Wilkins tells me you don't show much interest in our aviary. I think our budgerigars are such delightful little fowl.'

'Foul being the operative word.'

'Oh, Mrs Pyke, don't let's descend to that.'

'He's my dog and I intend him to stay here.'

Matron sighed, absently crushing a death certificate between her plump fingers.

'Can you prove he's your dog, Mrs Pyke?'

'You can see he loves me.'

'Dogs are naturally affectionate and Man is their master . . .'

'I am not a man.'

Matron reached for her white telephone.

'What's your husband's number?'

'I'm afraid I don't know.'

'I can always look it up in the directory you know.'

'Why don't you? You aren't paid expensive fees to economize on time and effort.'

Matron, who had been on the point of asking Elaine to pass her the directory, got up and walked to the bookcase and extracted it.

'One should be charitable,' she thought. 'She's had a nasty accident and her husband's a very clever man,' and stuck a fat finger in the first letter of the exchange.

Elaine listened hopefully as the 'phone in her house rang several times unanswered then her face fell as a jovial shout from Daniel rang through the receiver. She couldn't hear the rest of the conversation.

'He's coming tomorrow morning,' said Matron replacing the receiver. 'The dog will have to stay the night here. It's unfortunate, but it can't be helped.'

'He can sleep in my room,' said Elaine rising and taking Scott by the collar.

'Come on, darling, let's go to bed. We'll get you something to eat first.'

They went out and Elaine led the way into the kitchen where she took a Crown Derby bowl and filled it with water and gave it to Scott, and opened a cupboard, where on a plate was half a salami in silver paper. Elaine peeled off the paper and sliced the salami on to a plate and handed it to Scott who devoured it in seconds and drained his water-bowl. She put the dishes in the aluminium sink, switched off the light, and went upstairs. She tapped at Marjorie's door and Marjorie came out to kiss Scott good night. As she bent down she measured her knitting against him.

Alone in the bedroom she made Scott lie on the bed and smoothed handcream into his worn pads and took off her dressing gown and got into bed. She switched off the bedside lamp and Scott got in beside her.

At breakfast her hand shook as she shared the *Herald* with Marjorie and she spilled a cup of tea over Major Mallet, but this was attributed to his natural clumsiness. After breakfast she told Marjorie that she was going to take Scott in the garden and dressed in a straight red dress, went out, past the pool and into the bougain-villaea. She had to bend down to get through the thicket and laddered both stockings and scratched her face. There was a small gap in the wall that she had discovered a week ago and it led into an abandoned pigsty in the next door field. Elaine crawled through the gap and Scott followed through the nettles and the broken wall of the pigsty. It was fairly large, consisting of two rooms, but low ceilinged. A faint aroma of long departed pig hung round the damp walls and bits of straw on the floor. As time went on Elaine felt vaguely humiliated at hiding from her husband in a pigsty and she wandered boredly round the room talking to Scott. The faint notes of a handbell floated down the garden and dissolved among the tall nettles. Elaine went into the other room and saw on a heap of brown decaying straw the skeleton of a hen.

'Ladies and Gentlemen,' said Matron to her unattentive audience. 'We are rather concerned about Mrs Pyke. She seems to have disappeared. There is no cause for alarm, of course, but if any of you have any idea where she is I would be grateful if you would raise your hand.'

Out of the three raised hands Matron deigned to ask only one, for one belonged to a stone deaf schizophrenic and the other to Major Mallet. The answer of the favoured hand's owner was also disregarded on a count of ludicrousness.

'Well, thank you very much, everyone. If any of you see Mrs Pyke, could you ask her to speak to me. Thank you. Dismiss.'

Back in the lounge, Major Mallet mounted a card table and waved his arms for silence.

'Comrades,' he said. 'It's up to us to find Mrs Pyke. Who knows what appalling danger she may be in! If we don't rescue her no one will. Right! We will form into platoons and organize search parties. Paraplegics to the left – thank you – schizos to the right, and the rest of us led by me will tackle the bottom of the garden. Forward, March!'

When Daniel and the Matron, disturbed by a fierce and horrible noise, hurried to the window they saw a terrible spectacle. There was a burst of thunder and great grey and yellow clouds clashed about the sky, and heavy drops fell as the search party, led by Major Mallet brandishing an ebony club and uttering wild cries, burst through the french windows in a shower of broken glass and rushed on to the lawn. The metallic sun reflected off the wheels of wheelchairs as they rolled like great golden chariots over the flower beds, churning up the salvia and trailing broken strands of love-lies-bleeding.

'Onward!' shouted the Major and the cry was echoed by a dozen throats and in one case rose in a harsh scream that ended abruptly as a wheelchair rolled over its owner's throat.

'Casualty! Casualty!' shouted Major Mallet, tossing the wounded to one side. One lady had tied knives to her wheels and their blunt edges scraped the ankles of those who ran beside her.

Marjorie, fired by blood lust and love for her friend, led a small group of half a dozen paraplegics to the right round a clump of rhododendrons. Her strategy failed her here, so 'Faster! Faster!' she shouted as they wheeled round the rhododendrons and crashed into the back of Major Mallet's platoon and the air was filled with screams and groans and wheels and crutches cracked and flew about their heads. The riders held, horrified, to the sides of their chairs as, pushed by those behind, they rushed headlong down the garden, through the bushes and crashed into the wall behind. Some were torn from their perches by brambles and some bounced on the wire netting of the pond.

Elaine and Scott, with terror in their eyes, jumped up as Major Mallet hurtled through the pigsty wall.

'Expedition a hundred per cent successful,' he gasped

and fainted with a crutch through his leg and a wheel hung on his ear.

'Well. It looks as if they want the dog to stay,' said Matron to Daniel as the last doctor left.

'Yes.'

'I suppose it can be arranged, at some additional cost of course.'

So for the additional fee of ten guineas a week Scott was installed at Fairhaven Nursing Home among the infirm of mind.

The following day Daniel bent over his blonde secretary Joyce's typewriter and said:

'I wonder if you would care to have dinner with me tonight?'

They were sitting in the sun on the beach together, a
mile away from the hut, Leda in her red stretch nylon
swimming costume. A faint tan was just flushing the
surface of her skin and her mustard-coloured hair
blazed in the sun. The tide was right in and there were
miles and miles of deep green water warm on the surface
and cool underneath. Morris and Leda lay on the beach
all day, swimming from time to time. At about five
people began to depart and at seven o'clock they were
the only two left except for an old man in floppy wool
trunks and a tight red rubber skull cap, who dived with
the indignity of his white chest into each big wave. And
eventually he too came walking out of the sea, up the
pebbles on splayed feet, shaking the drops from his
chest and legs, and across the hard ribbed sand that
hurt his old feet and on to the soft ice-cream carton-
embedded sand and into a beach hut, from which he
later emerged radiant in orange shorts, pale green shirt
with its wide short sleeves just brushing his wrinkled
elbows, and white shining plimsolls, carrying his rolled
towel under his arm.

The sunset was beating down on the waves making a
golden path across the sea to the horizon, and the air
was growing cold. Morris walked out into the sea, then
felt the sudden cold catch under his arms and in a
moment he was swimming. He tried to follow the wide
sunset path but it burned into his eyes behind his closed

lids, and every time, swim as he would towards it, he opened his eyes, it was still on his right. He swam about on his back for a bit, then closed his mouth and breathed in and let himself sink with bent knees under the surface and down and down until he could see a green wall of water above his head and his wavering feet touched the sand beneath. Then he broke the surface and emerged through the green and gold, his wet eyes wide and stinging and his hair pushed back from his forehead, standing straight up, and a stream of silver bubbles burst from his parted lips. He swam back and lay for a moment in the shallows letting the little waves run over him and recede down his back. When he rejoined Leda he lay on the still-warm sand with a wet towel on his back and closed his eyes and lay exhausted in silence with his head on his folded arms for ten minutes. Leda, carefully manœuvring her towel, changed back into her jeans and one of Morris's shirts which strained a little at the buttons when she did it up. She watched the rise and fall of his white back and his legs, beneath the black trunks, pointing towards the sea.

'Come on, Morris, let's get back. I'm starving,' she said sprinkling a handful of sand down his spine.

'There's nothing to eat at home. Remember?' Morris lifted his eyes to her face and a sort of sob caught him in the throat so he was unable to think of food or drink.

'We'll have to go to that café up there,' Leda said, indicating with a wave of her hand some dark green tables and red and yellow umbrellas behind a circle of railings across the road.

'Got any money on you?'

'Look in my jeans pocket.'

She picked up his faded and salt-stained denims and

found three half-crowns and some small silver in the pocket. The rest of the money, the notes, was kept in a special zip pocket in his leather trousers which were hidden in the hut.

'We can have a proper meal – look, we're loaded.' Morris, unable to think of food or drink and his mouth dry with love for her, nodded as he placed his legs in his jeans over the dried sand and fastened his belt and rolled up the swimming things and towel and put them in the duffel bag, and they walked on legs slightly stiff from swimming and the sun across the warm tarmac and up to the café. It was called the Pavilion Café and Morris sat at one of the green tables, shielding his face with a newspaper he found on the chair, while Leda, putting on an old pair of sunglasses she had found in the sand, went into the Pavilion. Sitting at the table with the last of the day fading through the railings Morris suddenly felt very sad and had an urge to tell Leda how much he loved her in case it was soon too late – which he felt it might be, and his hands sweated in his pockets and writhed among the crumbs and fluff.

When she came out she was smiling above the steam that curled from her loaded tray. A young sailor came out after her with a bottle of coke. For a moment he hovered as if about to join them, then seeing Morris's look decided against it and sat at a table near them.

'Did he speak to you?' asked Morris.

'He offered to carry my tray; that's all,' said Leda in a way that made him ashamed of not being in a position to carry the tray for her.

'Do you still love me, Leda?' he asked taking the white plate of bacon, eggs and chips she handed to him and the thick cup of tea.

'Of course I do. I wouldn't be here if I didn't, would I? Do you still love me?'

'You know I do. I hate to see you do things, like carrying trays, but at the moment it can't be helped, can it? If that bastard doesn't stop looking at you I'm going over there to sort him out.'

'Don't be silly, Morris. Anyway he thinks you're my little brother.'

'Yes,' thought Morris. 'Yes, that's part of the tragedy of it all,' and he dipped his lips into the burning tea.

They walked home hand in hand, watching the tide's regress.

In the night Morris, waking and replacing his arm round Leda's neck, remembered the sailor's smiling face. Leda also woke once to the sound of heavy rain on the roof; she turned over and went back to sleep, and in the morning when she woke again she was cold and quickly dressed before Morris woke and lit the fire. She put her head out of the door and it was still pouring, the sand was thick and sodden, the dunes surrounded by yellow streams and the sky grey. She ran out and pulled a shirt from the concealed bush where it hung – it flapped wetly against her legs, so she hung it dripping over the table. She put her mac over her head and ran down to the sea and filled the tin and put it on the stove for tea. There was nothing to eat.

Morris lay asleep, his dark lashes peaceful on his white cheek and the dark circles round his eyes apparent in the grey light, his visible fist clenched and his mouth closed. Leda decided to let him sleep and while the water was boiling washed her face in the rain and combed her hair, the comb sticking in the salt and tangles. When the water was bubbling up the sides of

77

the tin she sprinkled in a handful of tea and stirred it
with a stick, then poured some milk and the remains of
the sugar in. Morris, when she woke him, did not smile
with sufficient appreciation of her efforts so she took
several mouthfuls before thrusting the tin into his half-
awakened hand and turned away while he drank it. The
tea was weak and the sugar did not cancel out the salt.
Leda turned just in time to see him grimace as he put
down the tin.

'It's your own fault if you don't like it. You could
easily afford a tea pot.'

'I told you I don't want to waste money on necessities. We're going to need it when we get to France.'

'When!'

'What do you mean "When"? I've been trying,
haven't I?'

'Yes, dear.'

'What do you mean, "Yes dear"?'

'Stop saying "What do you mean" like that. I was
only agreeing with you. I mean all these days you've
been lying on the beach you've probably been searching
the sea for a boat or maybe you've been swimming out
to submarines.'

Morris banged down the tin on the table and dragging them out from the hiding place in the wall, put on
his leather trousers. He took five shillings in silver
from the pocket and threw it at Leda saying:

'Here. Get yourself a tea pot.'

'I don't want a tea pot. It's you that's complaining,
not me. I'm quite content to live in squalor.'

Morris thrust his head through the neck of his shirt
and went out banging the door and saying, 'I'm going
for a walk.'

'Wait for me!'

'No. You better stay at home and clean up some of this squalor.'

He slammed the door and the piece of broken glass fell to the floor. He just gained the safety of a sand dune when a shoe came flying past where his head had been. Leda was going to go after him but she retrieved her shoe instead and went back inside. Alone in the hut she made no attempt to tidy up. She took a copy of *Woman* and sat over the fire reading. Half an hour later, looking up to find a biro for the crossword she saw that the fire had burned down and the sun was reflecting off the broken glass and making the dull red sticks of the fire look duller. She broke another couple of legs off the old chair and put them on the stove and decided to do some washing. A wet little heap of Morris's shirts and a skirt and blouse lay under the window where the rain had blown in under the tarpaulin. Leda picked them up and put them in her duffel bag and went out. The sun hit her in the eyes and the washed sand felt cool beneath her feet. The sea, full of rain, made no noise.

As she hung a pink shirt of Morris's on a branch of the dead bush a slight sound behind her made her turn. She screamed and stood staring for a minute into those terrible vacant grey eyes floating disconnectedly in the wet face. He had been out in the rain, his hair was flattened and water lay among the stubble of his chin. Leda grabbed the duffel bag and for a second hesitated between the hut and the sea while he stood smiling at her, his hands jerking and laughter dribbling wetly from the corner of his dark mouth, then ran towards the sea. The bag jolted against her legs and she tripped, dropped it and ran on and looking back saw him fall over it. She tried to increase her speed but her legs were already tired and she had to force them to run over the sand. She realized she was heading straight for the sea and so changed at a right angle to the right and went on running. Once she looked back and saw him coming, the duffel bag clasped to his chest with both arms, his gaunt legs churning in filthy flannels and his feet sprouting from broken plimsolls.

Half a mile away on a part of the beach they had never visited Leda could see a group of people and beyond them more people. A stitch was searing her side when she finally came within yards of them and her breath coming in great rasps which turned to sobs as a lump of sand struck her in the back of the neck. She slowed down to a fast walk and her pursuer ran a few more feet then did the same. Impeded by his plimsolls he was still several yards behind her. She gained the sanctuary of a more crowded part of the beach and walked among towels and deck-chairs until she was between two picnics and flopped down on the sand with her head on her arms and lay expecting at any moment a hand on her shoulder and a wet laugh in her ear. But when after a while she lay unmolested and the only laughter was the laughter of children she raised herself up and looked around. He was nowhere. She stood up but his ragged head couldn't be seen against the blue sky and his legs disfigured no deck-chair. Leda wondered what the time was, so she asked a woman who told her it was twelve-twenty. She decided to risk going back to the hut; she wanted to see Morris; and started walking when she realized she had no idea where she was or which direction to take – she seemed to remember vaguely running from the right but as she thought she recognized a formation of dunes to the left she walked towards it. When she reached it there was no familiar landmark only more dunes, reeds and eventually some boats. Leda now felt panic bumping her heart; she was alone again and lost on a deserted part of the shore and his hand might grab her ankle from any dune; and she ran back the same way as she had come, tears blurring her vision so that she trod on a piece of stick and fell clutching her feet and where a patch of blue Viper's Bugloss burned in the sand sank down and cried.

Here the sound of the sea was louder and she lay alone on the white sand under the hot Sussex sky beside the Viper's Bugloss burning and not being consumed, and the broken neck of a green bottle, through which the sun's rays reflected like petrol, and after a while she fell asleep. A gull's leg protruded stiffly from the side of a dune, its web splayed and opened as if inquiring for its fellow.

When she woke some hours later with a stomach-ache she shivered in her thin matelot T-shirt because all that remained of the day's heat was a few red rags in the grey sky. The tide had gone out, leaving a wet expanse where gulls plucked stones from the smooth sand, their feet making little sucking noises as they walked and orange red and olive shanks opposing the shallows and cries pervading the loneliness of the sky. She got up and stretched her legs which felt heavy and taut at the knees and tried to decide in which direction to go but couldn't and stood helplessly with the wind blowing through her T-shirt, staring at the empty beach. It looked sinister in the fading light with the dark patches of reeds and the stark dunes which could hide a man. She picked up a stick and tossed it over her shoulder to see in which direction it would point – it fell to the left but the left looked so forbidding that she started walking to the right. Above the beach was a marsh and she didn't want to get too near it, imagining the deadly squelch underfoot and no one to hear her screams as the black mud filled her mouth, except perhaps him and he would, holding onto a firm root, push her head under with his foot, and the terrible wet blackness before suffocation stopped her struggling and the black slime oozed into her burst and collapsed lungs.

She started running and thought she felt rain on her face, first a thin scattering, then long drops fell slanting in front of her, soaking the sand and her T-shirt. With a great clash of beaks and wings and voices the birds rose and flew inland over the marsh.

Running through the rain until her clothes were soaked to her skin Leda saw a dark shape in front of her and slowed into a walk in case it was a sleeping man. She approached it cautiously and after ascertaining that it was neither Morris nor the tramp, saw that it was an old upturned rowing boat. She felt it with her foot – the timber was rotten, and by pushing with all her strength at the stern she managed to raise it sufficiently to see that there was nothing inside it. She dropped it again and banged at what had been the floor with her shoe until she had made a hole about five inches across, then lifted it again and crawled inside. She turned round so that her face was near the air-hole and lay down. It was very dark so she pulled at the crumbling wood to widen the hole and a shower of decaying splinters fell on to her face. The rain was beating down on the wooden walls and coming through the air-hole. She turned on her side to avoid it and tried to sleep. She lay in the darkness for an hour or two and slept a bit, losing all count of time. Then when she thought it must at last be morning she pushed the boat up with her shoulders and crawled out. Black clouds were racing past the yellow moon and it was obviously not later than one o'clock. She went back into the boat in despair and fell asleep with the moon shining through the air-hole on to her worn-out face.

When Morris left the hut that morning, in addition to being upset by the quarrel with Leda, he was obsessed by the fear that Deirdre McGovern had betrayed him. He had no means of contacting her. He dared not go into the town so he walked along the beach, bored and worried, cutting at the rushes with a stick. He was also afraid of the effect the running away would have on Leda's parents. He realized it would greatly jeopardize his chances, for unknown to the Teagardens senior he had every intention of marrying their daughter. Mrs Teagarden anyway, whom he hated ever since he had heard her say 'Pity is akin to love, Leda', would do all in her power to oppose the match. He could imagine D. K. McGovern denouncing him to reporters, selling the story of the schoolgirl caught up in a hideous crime to the *News of the World*, and triumphant upon the witness stand.

After walking for about half an hour he became very hungry, and decided to risk going into the town for something to eat and something to eat for Leda, so he turned back and directed his steps towards the shops. On the way he was thinking what he would buy – peas, carrots, beans, potatoes, cherries, strawberries, raspberries, apples, pears, bananas, guavas, chocolate, cake, biscuits, milk. As he entered the shop with its smell of cheese and tea he thought that two women standing at the counter stopped talking. Unnerved, he forgot what he wanted and stood in the sudden silence and ordered a tin of baked beans and a pint of milk, then as talk resumed he remembered and packed the supplies in a carrier bag. The shopkeeper was looking at him very hard and hesitated when he handed him the money, and the women were staring at his leather trousers. When he left the shop he started walking as fast as he could, looking natural. He had not felt fear like that since Deptford and his face felt cold and sweaty; he forced himself not to look behind and walked quickly to the corner. He turned to the right just in time to see a man going into the 'phone box – he couldn't see if it was the shopkeeper but he was sure he recognized the grey overall. He kept walking past the shops and pushed his way through the crowded pavements until he came to a Woolworth's. A woman, entering in front of him, let the door swing back in his face so he walked between the counters holding a handkerchief to his bleeding nose. He didn't dare to go back to the hut in case he led the police there so he stood by the weighing machine at the door wondering what to do. A policeman passed slowly on his beat and Morris hid behind a rack of plastic macs for what seemed hours before he dared look out, until a woman pulled back the macs to select one, saw him and gave a little scream, causing heads to turn in their direction. He caught sight of himself in a mirror above the sweet counter and was shocked at the grey and bloody face and did not for a moment realize it was his. He spat on the corner of his handkerchief and tried to wipe some of the blood away but people were

84

staring so he made for the exit, holding the heavy
carrier bag half across his face. He walked down the
road thinking that everyone recognized him and were
running to 'phone boxes to contact the police. He saw a
public convenience on the other side of the road and
crossed through screaming brakes and lorries and went
into the gents. There was no attendant and he washed
the dried blood from his face and the sweat and put his
head under the tap. There was a hot air hand-drier in
the corner and he put the carrier bag down beside it
while he dried his hands in the warm airstream, then
his face. He hesitated for some minutes at the foot of
the stairs, reading a poster, then when a man and little
boy came down the steps he climbed up slowly, looking
carefully round before finally emerging, and seeing a
police car turned and ran down again. He leaned against
the wall, the white tiles and the sound of the running tap
making him feel faint. The bright poster on the wall
bulged and blurred in front of his eyes and he heard
dimly the voices of the little boy and his father recede
up the stairs. A door in a cubicle of opaque glass opened
and the attendant came out and looked at him and a
faint smear of blood on the basin. 'You all right, son?'
Morris nodded and went up the stairs. The patrol car
had gone and he walked quickly along the street the
same way as he had come. It was only after he had gone
a hundred yards and was outside Woolworth's again
that his arms felt curiously light and empty, and he
realized he had left the carrier bag behind. He heard a
shout behind him and turning saw the lavatory attendant standing on top of the steps waving and gesticulating at him. He pretended not to hear, and although he
knew it was stupid, started to run and ran blindly

bumping into people and knocking things out of their hands, not stopping when an old-age pensioner fell at his feet, past the shop where he bought the food, past the telephone box, down the lane, over the marsh and across the rushes and railway track to the hut. He leaned panting against the wall for some seconds, too weak to open the door and kicked it feebly. But Leda did not answer. He pushed it open. The place was empty, two half-burned chair legs lay on the fire and a magazine on the floor. The tin stood half-filled with cold tea, a salt scum on the surface. He went out and stood on a high dune searching the beach and sea for her but there was no sign and no answer to his hoarse shouts. Only a pink denim shirt hung fading in the hot sun from a broken branch of the dead bush. Morris sat down on the sand, leaning against the wall, to wait, but he couldn't and had to keep getting up and walking round the hut and climbing on the dune to look for her. Suddenly he saw that the duffel bag wasn't in its usual place under the table. His heart slowed down and he could feel it pounding as he stood with one hand leaning on the table and knew she was gone.

He stood there for some minutes, not moving and breathing heavily. Then his head crashed to the table and tears splashed out of his eyes and mixed with the blood from his nose which had started bleeding afresh so that when he ran out of the hut, his face was all bathed and smeared in tears and blood. He ran along the beach calling 'Leda Leda Leda' but there was no answer except the hot sun beating down on his head and crying and itching his face. At last, exhausted, he lay down in the sand and tried to think constructively. Leda must either have left as the result of the morning's

quarrel or the police had already been to the hut and
arrested her. He did not think the latter likely as they
would have left someone there to wait for him. He
doubted whether Leda would go home because (a) she
had no money, which would necessitate going to the
police and (b) police questioning when she got back.
Therefore she must be somewhere either in the town or
on the beach, in which case she would return to the hut
sometime.

He went back to the hut to wait but as he approached
he looked up and saw two figures in dark blue crossing
the marsh. Crouching down, he ran into the hut, threw
the tin out of the window, poured the tea over the fire
and kicked it out and grabbed his jeans and a shirt from
the table and was looking round once more frantically
when he saw something bright lying in the corner. He
picked it up. It was Leda's locket, and he put it round his
neck. He ran out, slammed the door behind him and
grabbed his pink shirt off the bush, and still crouching
ran under cover of the ridge of dunes as far along the
beach as he could before falling on his face. That night
it rained heavily and he woke next morning soaked and
hungry and before nine o'clock he had walked, feeling
intensely ill in mind and body, to a populated part of the
beach, where he sank against a breakwater and closed
his eyes.

When Leda awoke that morning, and stretched her stiff
legs and numb feet against the stern of the boat, and
emerged into the sunlight she was also very hungry.
She chewed a piece of rotten wood as she put on her
shoes. Then when she stood up she saw in the distance,
half a mile through the haze, a puff of smoke, then

another, and realized with a great burst of joy that it must be the railway near the hut. She ran diagonally up the sand and slowly opened the familiar door expecting to see Morris, loved and lovely, asleep on the table. The entire room had been overturned and the table lay on its back with the bench thrown across it and the door had been wrenched off the stove and the heap of firewood kicked about the floor. Morris and his belongings were gone. She couldn't believe he had been arrested and thought that the tramp must have gone back and wrecked the place out of revenge, and Morris, returning, had thought she had done it, and left. If the police had been there she knew they would have waited for her. She heard the faint sound of a car and going out, saw a black police car driving down the lane to the marsh; so she fled and spent that night and the next in her boat, living off food bought from the stall with the five shillings Morris had thrown at her.

Morris sat up and a hot red and yellow flush rushed up his neck and red and yellow shapes beat behind his burning eyes. He hung his head over the breakwater with his eyes closed for some minutes while apparent death beat in his hollow ribcage and his stomach heaved up to the base of his throat.

When he opened his eyes he was looking at an old man who lay on the sand beside two tethered donkeys. 'Feeling better, mister?' he said. 'Here, I'll give you a hand,' and he pulled Morris over the breakwater beside him and put the neck of a bottle between his pale lips. Morris felt sick again at the smell of whisky from the bottle and which pervaded the old man, but as the whisky burned down his throat and into his empty stomach he felt better and smiled at the old man as he returned the bottle.

'How did you know I was a mister?' he asked.

'I've been in show business, so I know. You're one of the lucky ones. I've seen them with heads as big as their bodies and legs as thick as your back.'

'Nice donkeys.'

'I suppose they are – for those that like them. I've got better things to do than hang round here all day.'

'Why don't you hire a boy to look after them?'

'You can't trust boys.'

'You can trust dwarfs, though. Remember the old saying, "as loyal as a dwarf"?'

'I can't say that I do. I take it that you're asking for the job.'

'Yes.'

'How do I know I can trust you? Have you any references?'

'The only reference I can give you is a strong pair of hands, an honest heart and the loyalty of a dwarf.'

So it was that Morris was employed as donkey boy by Mr Collins and his duties commenced from that moment. He led the donkeys up and down the beach, faint with hunger in the afternoon sun, with fat knees jolting his shoulders as he walked and his socks gradually filling with sand. At five past five Mr Collins returned unsteadily and placing an arm round either donkey's neck suffered himself to be led to the paddock.

Morris rubbed down the donkeys and fed and watered them. A blister throbbed on his heel and his head ached and when Mr Collins handed him a pound he received it gratefully as well as instructions to start work at ten o'clock the following morning. 'Here is my address, come and see me at five o'clock.' Morris thought that taking the job would both enable him to watch for Leda and also people would get accustomd to his face and think of him just as the donkey boy. He decided to postpone the trip to France until Leda could come with him.

He bought a Pepsicola, four hot dogs and two bars of chocolate from a stall – he dared not enter the town – and took them to a secluded place beside a broken breakwater half a mile from the hut. As he approached he kept closing his eyes and hoping that when he opened them a wisp of cloud would have changed to smoke above the chimney. He lay down to keep a watch on the hut and put a hot dog in his mouth and bit off the end but found it almost impossible to swallow, so he drank half the Pepsicola and tried again but the roll and sausage felt like lead bumping down his throat. He fell asleep with Leda's locket in his hands.

He worked for Mr Collins for two days and on the second morning at about twelve-thirty he saw walking towards him a woman as it were surrounded by children, but his eyes didn't linger on them. She was wearing a short red skirt beneath which lightly walked white legs. 'White legs,' he thought. 'How I have been tormented.'

As she organized the money for the children's rides a wedding ring flashed on her fumbling white finger and a sixpence fell in the sand. As Morris retrieved it and handed it to her and she stooped to take it she looked at him hard and said, 'Haven't I seen you somewhere before?'

'Perhaps you saw my picture in the paper.'

'Perhaps,' she agreed laughing to conceal the fact that she had taken him for a child and obviously not remembering where she had seen him and thinking he was joking. She sat down to wait while the children rode and when he had delivered them safely back, thanked him. About three o'clock they left the beach. Morris watched her go, and standing on a donkey's back discerned her red skirt entering a house not far above the beach.

After seeing Mr Collins he took a spade which he had found abandoned in a drowning castle and walked back along the promenade towards the low pink-washed house he had seen her enter. But, when he reached the gate he hesitated, realizing the children would soon be up, and went back to his hiding place and changed his shirt for a blue denim one. At eight o'clock it was cool and he walked through the perfume of night-scented stock to her door. When she opened it he said to her surprised and remembered face: 'Your little girl left her spade on the beach, so I brought it round.'

'That's awfully kind of you! But I'm afraid it's not one of ours.'

'Isn't it? I'm so sorry. I was sure it belonged to your little girl.' And with an apologetic smile he turned and began walking down the path.

'Wait a minute. Won't you come in for a bit? It was awfully nice of you to come all this way.'

Morris followed her over stone floors to a big room with a view of the sea. 'Would you like something to drink? Oh – I'm afraid there's only lemonade.'

'Lemonade would be fine.'

She returned with two tall glasses of lemonade and the ice cubes clinked as she set them on a low table.

'My husband,' she said, 'is in Rangoon,' sipping from her glass and looking at him over the rim.

When he discovered her name was Carol he was very disappointed for it was a name he had always hated; then, as he got used to it, what had been for years the representative of all he hated in a girl reminded him of Christmas and birdsong in fir trees and the sun shining on the holly-red of her skirt and her snowy legs.

She put on a record of *Eine Kleine Nachtmusik* and as a horizontal red bar faded in the west they talked in the greying light. It was decided that Morris should sleep downstairs and at eleven-forty Carol said good night as she spread him a blanket on the sofa. He took off his shirt and stood in front of the window for a bit. Then walked upstairs to what he hoped was her room. He closed the bedroom door and it was dark except for her white body. She had on only a black bra. 'I just came to say good night properly,' he said and put his arms round her, and she said, 'You can stay for a bit if you like.' Suddenly waking from half sleep he heard a child retch into the night upstairs and he thought, 'Go on – retch, retch,' but he finally got up and changed its sheets and washed its face and hands and even kissed the warm fetid cheek. Then he sat on the stairs and cried for Leda, until his eyes were sore and he was shivering so hard he could scarcely crawl back to her warm side where she lay sleeping like a Mexican and her four children slept above her.

In the morning he rose in the white light of four o'clock, unable to sleep, and walked through wet thistles and over the broken stone wall to the beach. The tide was half a mile out and he walked across the hard ribbed sand and wormcasts and shells to the water. When it was up to his knees he stood in the light water while gulls screamed about his head and looked back at the house. Beyond those black windows lay Carol among the tumbled sheets with one arm behind her head. A thrush burst from the thistles and flew like smoke across the chimney. The cries of the oyster-catchers and roseate terns and brown young gulls made him realize he was hungry and he had been standing while the cold sea washed over his feet for half an hour.

On the way up the beach he saw a gaunt dead cormorant tangled in a branch of driftwood; when the tide returned it would get washed out to sea. Morris picked up a piece of broken cuttle fish and put it in his pocket for Leda's budgerigar, then realizing he would probably never see it or her again hurled it back towards the sea and ran with dead sea-urchins cracking under his feet up the sand, across the road and over the wall.

When he pushed open the kitchen door he heard baby's cries and made himself a peanut butter sandwich. As he wiped the knife on his trouser leg and replaced it in the drawer, light reflected off the blade and pale sunshine was beginning to fall across the floor. When he awoke an hour or so later she was sitting up in bed with a bottle at the baby's mouth.

'I've made a cup of tea,' she said looking at him with a sweet early morning smile through heavy eyes. An envelope with bright foreign stamps and a Rangoon postmark lay half under the pillow. He lay drinking his tea, from a pink mug, watching her while the baby's mouth opened and closed like a flower on the bottle.

'I saw a dead cormorant on the beach this morning.'

'Yes, it has come in on every tide since Saturday.'

She replaced the baby in its cot and came back to bed. Morris put his arms round her and pulled her down to him but the feet of children were heard at the door and two girls and a boy entered quarrelling, the boy running forward to tell first, and they sat and bounced on the bed and plucked at the covers. Morris turned on his side in disgust and closed his eyes. 'Can't you send them away?' he muttered.

'They always come in the mornings,' said Carol.

'Why should we go away? It's not your bed – it's Mummy's.'

'And Daddy's.'

'And it's not your house.'

He went back to sleep again. When he woke the bedroom was empty and the sun blew in a salt shaft through the open window on to the bed. He carried his socks and shoes into the bathroom and washed off the dry sand and put them on. He went downstairs to find his shirt. A big teddy bear was lying on the floor wearing it. He also washed his face and combed his hair with a yellow comb he found on the basin.

In the kitchen she was standing in jeans in front of the stove frying eggs while the children sat round the table eating cereal and shouting. The jeans looked as if they had once been her husband's, who now stood in khaki shorts and a string vest and sun-helmet, directing bridge-building operations in Rangoon; they were tight across the hips and fairly loose on the legs, rolled up at the calves. Morris looked round the table and mentally tabulated: one had a lump of Weetabix on its chin, one's nose was running, one was examining a dirty plaster on its elbow and the baby was crying, sitting up in a carrycot with a wet rusk smeared about its face. He turned away as he ate his fried egg to the accompaniment of the infinitely depressing sound of burnt toast being scraped over the sink.

At last the children, two of them crying because their towels were wet, were sent to the beach. Carol cleared the table and Morris, standing on a chair, washed up.

'I must just rinse out these nappies,' she said, lighting a cigarette.

'I've got to go to work,' said Morris, stretching up to kiss her extended face. As she held him to her he smelled a faint scent of salt, shampoo and lavender.

'See you later?' she called, waving a sudsy hand from the doorway. Morris smiled and nodded as he went through the gate.

He went to the field and filled the bucket from the tap and fed and watered the donkeys, and while they mouthed the dry oats ran a peremptory brush over their thick tangled coats, and they looked up at him with eyes fringed with lashes and solidified tears. He put on their bridles and led them down to the beach. There were already quite a few people out. Morris hitched one donkey to the breakwater and mounted the other and galloped along the beach to the left, searching among the people. Then he changed donkeys and repeated the process to the right – expedition a hundred per cent unsuccessful. He stood on a donkey's back looking out to sea for any sign, floating hair, a white extended arm, but the sea was empty of all but fish and gulls. Morris and the donkeys trotted, cantered and walked till one o'clock when he led them back to the field for their lunch hour. This was his own idea. He went into the shed to get the bucket and tripped over the handle of a rake and fell, hitting his knee on something hard. He thought it was a stone and kicked at it with his foot dislodging the straw to reveal something that shone dully like green glass. He stooped down and scraped away the straw and picked it up – it was a full bottle of whisky. He concealed it delightedly with his handkerchief and quickly took the bucket, filled it and gave it to the donkeys to drink. He came back and lay face downwards, head extended towards the sea, on the hot sand. A discarded ice-cream slowly melted by his head.

He decided not to go back that afternoon; the donkeys would enjoy half a day's rest in the heat and thistles, alone in the broken down field. Donkeys whose hooves were worn with others' pleasure, who walked delicately on the early wet sand and stood dewy-fetlocked in the paddock at night while their riders, the sand rubbing from their quiet feet, slept in hotel and caravan and private house. He took a drink from the bottle and another two or three, concealing it with his cradled arms, lest someone take it from him, and lay forward as the whisky burned his throat and the sand burned his face, drinking half the bottle quickly.

He remembered with pain and tears Leda crouched with the bunch of twigs in her hand, blowing their fire and feeding it with strips of paper while smoke poured up round the blackened tin of baked beans, and chips in the rain at Deptford, and evenings discussing plans with Manny Margolis and Tom while she sat on the bed reading a magazine and swinging her leg while her shoe slipped from her foot and her beer stood flat and stale in its glass and the finished record scratched round on the hot turntable. Or last winter, sitting on her legs in black tights slightly wrinkled at the knees, crying with exasperation and rubbing her chilblains while she tried to force her shoe over her swollen heel.

Where was shen ow? Laughing with what sunburned sailor at a café table, leaning across to feel his muscles straining in the short sleeves of his white T-shirt, the sun glinting on the short hairs on the back of his neck, while the straws in the empty coke bottles leaned intimately towards each other?

Morris raised the bottle to drown the thought. He put his hand inside his shirt and lifted her locket spinning on its thick silver chain over his head and opened it to reveal where, against their smiling faces, he had lain the only letter she had written him. For how many half hours had she sat clicking a Biro against her teeth, or may be it only took three minutes, while she wrote on lined paper:

Dear Morris,

I am afraid I can't see you any more. I have met someone else. Please forgive any unhappiness I have caused you. I will never forget you and hope you won't me. I have sent Golly back as a souvenir.

Love Leda.

He had found the golliwog he had won at Blackheath Fair sitting on his doorstep early one morning with dew in his black fur hair and a note tied to his paw with a pink bow. As he stumbled up the stairs trying to untie it, a pint of milk slipped from under his arm and flowed disregarded through the broken glass while he read the letter which he did not really need to read. This was the first of their four partings.

Leda, crying, while Ray Charles sang and her thin sister died of cancer in Lewisham Hospital. He remembered her sitting up in the high bed with a speck of blood on the frill of her nylon nightdress while bright banks of daffodils and tulips stood on the radiator.

And Leda playing Ludo at his grandmother's, back from a week in Haly, her sunburned hands with white interstices between the fingers moving among the coloured counters so that he wanted to kiss them and he put out his hand to touch hers on the board and his grandmother accused him of cheating.

The flames dying in a gas fire, the shadow of her hair.

He tipped the last drops down his throat. He looked into the sun and great yellow suns burned behind his closed eyes and the sand began to spin, at first gently, then the whole beach was turning like a vast roundabout and he closed his eyes again as deck-chairs spun round on the shore, hitting the wall and the edge of the sea. He was drowning in sand and the cries of children caught in the revolving blue sky deafened him.

It stopped and he lay panting, his fingers dug up to the knuckles in sand.

Then he saw her. She was far out at sea, she had seen him, she was waving! He ran into the sea. It was up to his waist and he began swimming strongly although the waves were blurred and there was a ringing in his ears.

Then he lost sight of her and behind him, cast backward by a current, bobbed a branch of driftwood.

He was swimming easily now and the roaring had stopped. He smiled through watery lips to think how she would be waiting laughing behind the next wave. But he wasn't swimming now, he was lying on the water and the next wave went right over him. Oh, Leda, don't you remember the way I used to smile?

[18]

The sun at two o'clock beat down on the crowded sand as Leda, with her jeans in pink rags round her legs and grains of sand rubbing in her blisters, walked painfully along the shore and searched between the deck-chairs for Morris. The bright striped canvas hurt her heavy eyes and when she turned away orange and yellow stripes jumped in front of her. As she dragged her fiery feet along she trod on a child's sandcastle. It was not so much an accident, as she saw it, but lacked the ability or desire to avoid it and so it crumpled between her feet. The little boy jumped up and down screaming and his father threw a tin spade at her which caught the side of her foot and cut it, making a dismal clogged river through the encrusted sand.

She saw a crowd standing some distance further along the shore and people sitting watching on the promenade wall. Through the hazy air she could see among them at least a dozen dark heads that might belong to Morris so she walked slowly towards them. As she approached she heard an accordion playing and voices singing. She stood on the edge of the crowd between a singing Irish-woman and a group of boys who had come to mock. When one of them smiled at her she moved round to the other side of the crowd, too tired to smile and far too exhausted to make the effort of speaking to strangers. A man of, at a conservative estimate, fifty-seven, with a knotted handkerchief on his head, stood on a wooden box, playing an accordion, and as he stamped his foot to the beat, sweat jumped from his eyes and rolled down his baggy grey suit above the sound of the sea. Round him marched half a dozen children singing with actions:

> 'I'm in the Lord's army
> Marching to Victory.
> I'm too young to
> March with the infantry,
> Ride with the cavalry,
> Shoot with the artillery.
> I'm too young to
> Swoop on the enemy,
> I'm in the Lord's army.'

Leda sat down to watch although she felt blushes for the monstrous participants flushing her face and the back of her neck. The Evangelist, whose name was Uncle Harry, stepped down from his box and took the hand of a girl aged four with custard-coloured curls, and in a Glasgow voice proclaimed as he lifted her on to the box, 'Boys and Girls, Ladies and Gentlemen, Fellow Sinners, wee Linda here would like to sing a song for Jesus. What would you like to sing, Linda? One, two, three? Right you are then, Linda. Uh one, uh two . . .' and Linda stood singing and swaying backwards and forwards in her nylon dress while her wee feet in their yellow socks stamped up and down.

> 'One, two, three,
> The devil's after me.
> Four, five six,
> He's always throwing bricks.

101

Seven, eight, nine,
They miss me every time.
Allelulia. Allelulia. Amen.

Nine, eight seven,
I'm on my way to Heaven.
Six, five, four,
My cup is running o'er.
Three, two, one,
The devil's on the run.
Allelulia. Allelulia. Amen.

When the applause died and the tears from the corners of a few old eyes were wiped, wee Linda put her hands together, knelt down and said, 'Thank you for the world so sweet thank you for the food we eat thank you for the birds we eat thank you God for everything,' and skipped off the box. Uncle Harry patted her on the head and, he thought unobtrusively, pressed a sixpence into the sweaty wee palm, and Linda danced in her white sandals to an ice-cream man who stood on the promenade.

Leda watched all this with unseeing eyes, but when a lady in a sun-hat and a sleeveless dress exposing a burnt red neck and flabby arms began to sing 'The Old Rugged Cross', she looked down and drew with a twig in the sand, and was also looking down when the collection box passed over her tangled head. She had reached a state of despair, where she was a listless spectator of other people's fun, accepting each blow as inevitable, and completely without hope of seeing Morris again. She felt incapable of fears and felt that for her there was no breaking point. As she sat among the children singing of Jesus she accepted that her life would be a series of blunders and episodes of suffering, terminating in nothingness. She looked up and saw a man on the wall above her take out a yellow plastic tobacco pouch and a packet of papers and slowly roll a cigarette, pouring the tobacco carefully into the paper, licking the edge delicately with the tip of his tongue, and carefully rolling it into shape, tapping out the surplus on his lighter and returning it to his pouch.

'I am dying for a smoke,' thought Leda, and realized she had not had one for five days. And lying in front of her, not three feet away, but within the circle of marching children lay a long filter-tipped dog end. Even as she watched, wee Linda trod it into the sand. It was just visible, bent and flattened above a little heap of sand; she could have reached it and taken it but, aware of fifty pairs of eyes, could not move her arm. Then as some eyelids closed in prayer she, so nonchalantly it surprised herself, leaned forward and plucked it from its little grave. Then, turning to the man beside her, said without the effort of a smile between cracked lips, 'I wonder if you can give me a light,' and thanked him for his contempt as well as the short flash of sulphur and flick of his righteous wrist and the male hand momentarily held towards her though not in friendship. So the degraded among us are.

Suddenly the heads of the congregation turned like birds to the east, where an amphibious pleasure craft was plunging its snout through the shallows with children leaping around it, and as it wheeled spurting up the shore they raced after it and all along the beach children were running after it and the congregation rose, Leda with them, and ran, not knowing why, along the great wet tracks in the sand, with Linda singing her wee heart out on the box and no one caring.

'I shouldn't be doing this. I'm not interested,' Leda thought as her feet pounded the sand to the tune the accordion still jangled in her head.

> 'Have you got the sunshine smile?
> Have you got the sunshine smile?
> Wherever you may be
> Whoever you may see
> Always have the sunshine
> SMILE.'

'It will only be something horrible.' Now boys were hanging and clinging to the back of the boat and one who scraped his foot along the sand fell and lay disregarded. Two policemen were running down the steps and pushing the children back and pleading with the adults to move back. It was in vain, the crowd pushed forward crowding up to the sides of the boat.

'It's a little boy,' said a woman.

The red blanket was carried out but the white foot with a wisp of seaweed dragging from the toes was not a child's foot.

> 'Wherever you may be
> Whoever you may see
> Always have the sunshine
> SMILE.'

Leda fell forward into the blackness below the spades and swimming trunks and a castle hit her in the face.

When she was carried into the St John Ambulance

Hut the lady in charge saw a great bruise beginning to swell on her arm. 'She must have been walked on,' she thought. When she woke on a camp bed Leda felt a deep ache inside which she thought was perhaps hunger, so the first words she spoke as the ambulance lady bent over her and asked if she felt better were, 'I would like something to eat.' And the woman, recognizing her face from the blurred photographs in the papers, sent her assistant first to buy some food and then to telephone the police.

'You're safe with us, dear. We know who you are.'

Leda jumped up and ran towards the door and along the stone promenade although her feet slipped on the sand and her legs were refusing to follow and the blood beat against the walls of her head. She was overtaken after only a few feet, and with one arm drooping round her strong red neck in grey the St John Ambulance lady half dragged, half carried, her back to the hut.

A paper of cold chips was handed to her and on a shelf were a green salt and vinegar. 'Everything's all right, dear. You can stop running now.' Which was perfectly true as there was nothing left to run for.

'Yes. Pass the salt, please.' Although she was already choking on more salt than her eyes could manage.

THE END